Copyright © 2019 by Alexa B. James and Katherine Bogle

Cover Design by Katzilla Designs

First Edition — 2019

No part of this publication may be reproduced in any form, or by any means, electronic or mechanical, including photocopying, recording, or any information browsing, storage, or retrieval system, without permission in writing from Alexa B. James or Katherine Bogle.

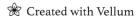 Created with Vellum

# Silver Shifter

## 1

### Her Wolf

# James & Bogle

# 1

## ARIANA

In the stands above my cell, the air crackled with excitement. The constant hum of voices and the familiar vibration of impatient feet pounding the bleachers had woken me from a dream I didn't let myself remember.

"Fight! Fight! Fight!"

The chant filtered down through the few cracks in the ceiling. I stood and shook off the last vestiges of the dream—flashes of blood and teeth—and stretched my limbs.

"Wakey, wakey," taunted a cruel voice. A figure strolled through the dimness outside my cell, running his club along the vertical bars. Each time it hit a bar, a loud bang echoed through the darkness.

Somewhere in another cell, a wolf whimpered pathetically. I didn't whimper. I bared my teeth and growled at the vampire.

He laughed harder, shoving the club through the bars to poke my protruding ribs. I snapped at the weapon, imagining what it'd be like to break his bones with my powerful jaws. Once his laughter died, I moved out of his reach and across the dirt floor of my small cage. My silver paws shone white against the packed earth on either side of my bowl as I leaned down to smell it, already knowing it was empty. The only way to get fed was to win.

As if to emphasize that truth, the crowd overhead erupted into cheers. Dust poured through the cracks in the ceiling as spectators stomped their feet. A few seconds later, my master's voice boomed in the ring. My heartbeat sped, anticipation charging my limbs when I heard my name.

It was my turn to fight.

"For tonight's entertainment, we have Ariana and Benjamin… in a fight to the death," Dante announced like the grand showman he was.

The crowd cheered.

I paced my cage, a growl building in my throat.

The vampire gave me one last sharp-toothed grin before unlocking my cell.

"Don't get your head ripped off," he said with a sneer.

He swung the cage door open and stepped back, keeping the bars between us. I snarled at him just for kicks, but I couldn't waste energy on a vampire. He may have been the one who had collected on my parents debt by taking our freedom, but killing him wouldn't let me live another day. Winning would.

I trotted down the short tunnel and emerged on the floor of the pit. The frenzy increased—spectators pounding the floor and screaming with bloodthirsty excitement. They'd soon get what they came for.

I trotted up to Dante like a trained dog, though he had long ago stopped treating me like a pet. I wasn't his dog anymore. I was his weapon.

"Please enjoy the fight, and don't forget to pay your debts, or you might end up here next." Dante winked at the crowd as if he were kidding. He wasn't.

The bloodstained concrete floor of the pit told the truth of the matter. Dante wasn't above throwing a human into the pit if they owed him. He called it a bonus for the spectators—a little something extra after the fight. At first, I hadn't wanted to kill a defenseless human, but I'd learned quickly. There were only two options in the pit: kill or die.

Without a word to me, Dante took his place in the spectator's box, a special enclosed seating area that extended over the edge of the pit.

My attention snapped away from my master and back to the tunnel I'd emerged from moments before. A clang alerted me to another cage opening. My cell was one of many, each filled with a beast unfortunate enough to owe Dante a debt. Tonight, a shifter would pay.

The bobcat that emerged from the tunnel brought

cheers, but I barely heard them. The moment I laid eyes on him, all thoughts turned to the kill. Cats were twistier than wolves, with sharper claws. But I was faster and stronger and had years of experience.

I leapt in before he could get his bearings, snapping at his throat. But he was surprisingly quick, and he leapt away. With a loud hiss, he bared his long fangs.

Somewhere in the stands, I heard shouts, but I couldn't look away for a second. A second was all it took to lose focus and lose a fight.

Benjamin didn't look away, either, not even when footsteps pounded on the walkway leading to the spectator's box overhead.

Renewing my focus, I leapt, sinking my teeth into the cat's side. He screamed in pain, spitting and raking his claws down my hip as he rolled under me. I sprang free, dropping the chunk of flesh I'd torn from his shoulder. We circled each other as shouts rang out overhead, a different kind of yelling than the rabid fans cheering for us to rip each other to shreds. That was what put food in my bowl, so I focused on that as I darted in for another attack.

Before I could make the next move, the cat leapt onto my back and sank his teeth into the scruff of my neck. A spear of panic shot through me. I rolled, crushing him beneath me long enough shake loose before darting away.

Behind me, I heard a man shouting.

"Stop, Ariana! You don't have to do this."

A man was foolish enough to jump into the pits? Or had Dante provided the distraction, hoping to amp up the excitement of the fight? I would deal with the man later, but I couldn't afford to lose focus on the bobcat. The man leapt in front of me as I dove for my opponent, but I swerved around him. Swiping at me with one hand, he just missed me as I gathered all my strength and leapt onto the bobcat. With my powerful jaws ready, I caught the cat by the throat, and before he could tear himself free, I braced my silver paws on his shoulders and wrenched with all my strength.

I heard his skull hit the floor behind me as his head rolled free. I dropped his body, blood spurting onto the cement.

Turning, I focused on the man. He must owe my master a debt. It was my job to collect.

He'd already stripped off his shirt, and now he quickly dropped his pants. To my horror, he dropped to all fours, and a wolf emerged from his body.

Two fights in one night? Two *fair* fights?

This was no bonus fight, no helpless human whose life I had to take if I wanted to keep my own. This was a big, strong, healthy wolf—one who outmatched me even when I wasn't leaking blood from a half dozen scratches and puncture wounds. This wolf had a thick, glossy coat and the rippling muscles of a well-fed animal.

Had Dante decided to get rid of me even though

I'd won dozens of fights and brought in more money than any other shifter he owned? He had to know this wasn't a fair fight.

My claws dug into the cement and my nostrils flared as the flames of anger burned through my entire body. With a roar of rage at the injustice, I leapt at the wolf.

## 2

## MAXIMUS

The stench of blood wafted through the walls even outside the fighting pits. I wrinkled my nose and resisted the urge to cover my nose and mouth. It had taken me three weeks to find the pits and get an invitation. Three weeks of agony knowing someone was stealing wolves from *my* territory and using them for their sick games.

A growl rose in my throat and I quickly squashed it. Though I wasn't the only shifter here tonight, I had to keep a low profile.

"The last fight starts in five minutes, everyone!" a voice called from up ahead.

I squinted through the darkness. If I didn't want those around me to see the yellow shift of my wolf eyes, I couldn't use them to peer through the darkness right now. With dozens of upper class supernaturals weaving through the dank stone corridor, I held back my urge to unleash the wolf inside.

The crowd shifted out of the corridor and through a steel door with a grated window in the top half. Beyond, bright fluorescent light illuminated rows of stands and a special viewing booth on the edge of a dark pit carved from stone.

I joined the flow of the crowd, exchanging a quick glance with one of my pack up ahead. Shira, my second-in-command, dipped her chin in a barely discernible nod before she slipped inside. I was quick to join the rest of the supernaturals here for the fight.

Once the first death match began, my team would make their move, closing in from the outside while Shira and a few others took over from within. No one was getting away tonight. The pit masters would pay for what they were doing to shifters.

The burn of anger blazed inside my chest, and I ground my teeth together.

*Kill*, my wolf urged. If it was possible, he was more pissed off than I was. Though I could be reasoned with and spend time forming a plan, my wolf wanted nothing but blood. Someone was in his territory, and he'd kill without a second's pause.

The crowd took their seats around the pit, shifting into the rows of stands ascending from the floor to a few rows high.

A man with black hair and a smug grin chatted with Shira beside the expensive viewing booth dipping just over the edge of the pit. From her strained smile, it was clear she wanted to tear his head off as much as I did. The mic in his hand indicated his status as a pitmaster or at least an announcer. Either way, he knew what went on here, and he allowed it.

I strolled around the opposite side of the pit, my fists clenched as I took a few calming breaths. It didn't help. Not with the copper tang in the air and the faint whimpers from somewhere below.

So many had died here. From the blood staining the concrete ten feet below, it had to have been dozens, maybe hundreds.

A clang from below had me leaning over the chain railing surrounding the dark chasm. A light flashed on from above, and I looked up just in time to see the announcer disappear from Shira's side and reappear in the bottom of the pit.

Warlock.

My nostrils flared, and I couldn't hold back my growl this time. Magic stained the air with a floral scent that turned my stomach.

"For tonight's entertainment, we have Ariana and Benjamin, in a fight to the death." The man grinned and tossed his arms out at his grand announcement.

I barely resisted the urge to shift into wolf form as the crowd roared around me.

From a dark tunnel in the side of the pit, a flash of silver fur made my blood run cold. My heartbeat sped, and my fingers closed around the chain railing.

No. It couldn't be.

A wolf, not gray, or white, but *silver* walked from the narrow passage, her head low and her eyes lit with bloodlust. She trotted to the center of the pit, stopping beside what I had to assume was her master.

The frenzy around me increased, and shoulders banged against mine as the crowd lurched forward to peer at the one creature I'd spent my entire life waiting for.

*The Silver Shifter.*

She was a creature of legend, one that only came around every hundred years. The last Silver Shifter, a dragon, had the gift of an oracle. She had left behind a string of prophecies about the next Silver Shifter—the one supposed to be the last.

But I didn't care about the prophecies and legends. I cared about the emaciated she-wolf below, because in that moment my wolf finally quieted, and one word came through the silence inside.

*Mate.*

Each Silver Shifter was meant to mate with the alpha of their pack, whichever shifter clan they were born to. This Silver Shifter, this beautiful wolf with a coat like liquid silver...she was *mine*.

The announcer teased the crowd a bit more, but I was hardly paying attention anymore.

A whine of worry came through the pack bond, and I glanced up to meet Shira's gaze. Her brown eyes were wide, and she gripped the railing with white knuckles. Shira could feel everything I felt. All the confusion, the concern, and the overwhelming need to claim and protect Ariana as my own.

I took a deep breath. I had to calm down and think rationally, but with my wolf suddenly howling for action, I was tempted to give in.

A loud clang made me freeze. I looked below in time to see a mangy bobcat slink out of the tunnel into the pit. I hadn't seen the announcer leave, but he was back in the spectator's box, a grin on his face as Ariana turned to face her opponent.

*Shit.*

The urge to protect my mate surged through my every muscle with an intensity I'd never known. It snatched my breath away and sent whines of concern flaring through my head. The pack needed orders.

*Everyone move in*, I commanded. The whines quieted, replaced with relief.

I pushed back the thoughts of my pack as shouts burst from below. Somewhere a door crashed in, and then my pack was inside.

Chaos erupted around me, replacing the frenzied bloodlust of the crowd with fear as they turned to run in every direction.

While my pack took care of the others, it was time for me to save my mate. Gripping the railing, I swung over. Wind rushed against my ears for a moment before I landed hard on the ground.

Ariana was already fighting the bobcat, her

powerful muscles bunching and tensing below her fur. Part of me was tempted to stop and watch, to see how strong my future mate really was, but the protective side of me won out as the bobcat launched itself onto my mate's back.

A growl rumbled in my chest and I took a step forward to throw that damn cat away from her, but in the next moment she had freed herself. Relief filled me until I saw the murder in her eyes. She was going to kill that cat.

My chest squeezed with panic as I dove between them both. I reached for Ariana, moving to grab her scruff and pull her away, but she was fast, and she leapt around me before I could get my hands on her.

I turned in time to see this small, emaciated wolf rip the head of the bobcat from its shoulders and toss it across the cement floor. I winced as it *thunked* against the ground and rolled into the shadows. Blood drowned the floor in a sea of red, but Ariana wasn't looking at her kill anymore.

Dappled in red spots and growling like a beast, Ariana met my his gaze, her silver eyes flashing with murder.

*Well, fuck.*

Before I realized what I was doing, I'd stripped off my dress shirt and tossed it onto the floor. Cold air licked my warm skin as I dropped my pants next. There was no fighting a wolf in human form. I had to shift, and quick.

Pulling my wolf to the forefront of my mind, I let him take control, shifting my body with a series of searing hot shots through my muscles and bones. The agony was gone in a second as I embraced my wolf form.

The scent of blood was even thicker, and my acute hearing picked up the rapid thump of Ariana's heart. I took a step forward, my claws clicking against the cement.

Ariana's nostrils flared, and her rage shimmered through the air with her snarl. I could nearly feel the heat of it as she bared her teeth and braced to leap.

My mind raced as I calculated her movements and tried to come up with a plan. Ariana was beyond listening, and she certainly wasn't getting any calmer with me in the pit.

Perhaps I should have waited, but there was no going back now.

Ariana leapt, and my wolf dove to the side. I felt the tremble of his half growl, half whine. He didn't want to fight her anymore than I did.

The silver wolf dove again, but I was quicker, leaping out of her way before her paws hit the floor. She turned another snarl on me, but I was already stalking away.

Did she not see that I didn't want to fight her? Could she not tell I was no threat?

A growl of frustration echoed in my mind, but I refused to unleash it or show any other kind of hostility toward Ariana. Hostility would only make her more wary.

We continued our dance, Ariana leaping, jaw snapping at my throat, while I dove out of reach. Each time, her nostrils flared and she pawed at the ground angrily. She wanted a fight. She wanted a kill.

My heart sank and my ears flattened back against my head as a terrible thought flitted through my mind. Had she gone feral? Was I too late? What if she'd been outside a pack for too long?

Every shifter knew that a lone wolf wasn't long for this world. Without a pack, a wolf slowly lost their mind until they were more beast than human. Only alphas could survive on their own, but an alpha without a pack would never feel whole, never be satisfied.

Ariana jumped again, and I matched the movement. Before I landed, she shifted her body in midair and tore off the ground, slamming her shoulder into my chest.

Wind huffed from my lungs, and I staggered, trying to get my feet under me.

Teeth sank into my neck, but I ripped free before Ariana could do any damage. I tried to put space between us, but she'd already jumped again, slamming into my side and forcing me against the wall.

A growl tore from my throat as I spun to face her, forcing all of my alpha dominance into my gaze.

A normal wolf would back down immediately,

knowing there was nothing they could do to overcome me. But Ariana didn't back down. Instead, she met my gaze with unwavering silver eyes and dove at my face.

I yanked my head just out of her reach.

So it was true. Ariana had gone mad.

I darted a few steps back, evading every swipe of her claws and snap of her teeth, but she didn't relent. If I didn't do something soon, I'd lose her for good. The shouts above were quieting, and if my pack saw another wolf attacking me, even the Silver Shifter, they might be tempted to intervene.

*"Keep out of this,"* I growled through the bond.

Before I could discern their answers, Ariana crashed into my chest, forcing me onto my side where she crouched on top of me and ripped at my flesh with her claws.

Pain slammed into my shoulder, and I snarled as I snapped at her face, not to hurt her, but to scare her into a retreat.

She didn't retreat. She was too far gone.

There was only one thing I could do. I had to bring her into the pack. If I could return her mind to the present—to the human form she might not have seen in some time—then there might be hope yet.

I only had one shot.

Growling, I slammed by back paws into her chest, throwing her off. I was on my feet before she'd landed, and I dove at her neck.

To force a pack bond, I needed to mix my blood

and hers. She'd be forced, if only temporarily, into the pack mind. It should be enough to pull her back to sanity.

Adrenaline coursed through my veins as I bit down on my tongue. Copper burst inside my mouth. I leapt, gripping her neck in my huge jaw, and clamped down hard enough to break the skin. The taste of a new blood flooded my mouth, but before I could pinpoint what exactly the undercurrent of that taste was, a new mind joined the pack bond.

Releasing Ariana, I shook my head and backpedaled as images flew across my mind.

*Blood, death, fangs, and a dark cell.*

This was Ariana's mind. This was my mate's life.

# 3
## ARIANA

I staggered back from the wolf, barely able to stay on my feet. I had been bitten many times, but nothing like this had ever happened. Words flashed in my mind, invading me.

*Mate.*

*Mine.*

*Alpha.*

Images flooded my head: images of a prophecy, a skinny silver wolf, and a huge wooden house. I whined, shaking my head. Someone was in my head, and my own memories flashed back at me like a mirror. Memories of my home in the cage, of dirt and blood and fighting.

*Shit! The fight.*

I would never win it like this. I fought to clear my head, lurching forward with bared teeth. The other wolf stared into my eyes, and I felt my growl turn to a whine, my head dropping as if my master had stepped on the back of my neck.

What had he done to me? This wolf had bitten me, but more than that, he must have injected me with some kind of poison.

And then the emotion swept over me, knocking me flat with the intensity—horror, desperation, and pity. My own emotions fought back against the intrusion, and I snarled at the pity he was forcing into me.

*Let out your human.*

I jerked my head up, startled by the thought that had crashed over me.

*My human...?*

The thought was as familiar as my cage, and yet, as forgotten as the life I'd lived before it. The wolf stepped forward, nudging my neck with his muzzle. He put both paws on my shoulders and stared into my eyes. With a series of jerks, he changed, right before my eyes, into a human.

"Let out your human," he said aloud this time.

Before I could think to snap at his exposed and vulnerable belly, my own body began to spasm and bunch. Seconds later, I sat in front of him in human form.

Everything in my body felt wrong. I was no longer myself, and yet, I was more myself than I'd ever been. My thoughts began to take more human form, too. I hadn't been in this body in...years. Now I sat before a man who was as naked as me, more bare than I'd ever been as a wolf. I threw my arms around my body, jerking back from the man who sat in front of me, his hands still on my shoulders.

I could still feel the mental intrusion, like a tongue was licking into my brain.

"Get out!" I screamed, grabbing my skull with both hands.

The man reeled backwards, grabbing his own head.

"Whoa, Ariana," he said, his voice gentle but firm. "I'm Maximus, and I'm not going to hurt you. You don't have to fight me. I've mixed my blood with yours, which has bonded you to my pack. We can't help feeling any intense emotion from you."

I jumped to my feet, scrambling back. I could feel my wolf inside, too, snarling to get out. She wanted to leap at the man's back as he turned and retrieved his clothes. He slipped into his pants, zipping them before turning to me. He held out a dress shirt, and his mind commanded me to step forward and take it.

The feeling of being compelled was unbearable, and he winced as I snatched the shirt and retreated. I turned away as he had, pulling my clumsy arms through the sleeves. It didn't fit me like fur, but it was better than the exposed feeling of bare skin, where every air current tickled almost painfully. Hugging the shirt around me, I stared at this Maximus. I could feel him, his worry and urgency, his trepidation about...me.

My wolf snarled to get free, but his command held her in check. I could tell she was stronger than me, but his mind was even stronger than her. I appreciated the sharp clarity of my mind after the years of fog and monotony where the only thought was survival and the only emotion was fear.

Trying to ignore the swirl of thoughts and feelings being imposed on me, I turned to Maximus and asked him the only pressing question.

"Are you my new master?" My voice was squeaky and weak with disuse, the words feeling foreign on my tongue.

"No," he said quickly. "I'm your alpha right now, which is why I can communicate clearly with you in wolf form."

"What's the difference?" I asked, tugging at the bottom of his shirt, which barely concealed my upper thighs. I wanted more coverage. I wanted my fur coat back.

A wave of anguish washed over me, and I almost cried out before realizing it came from him. It was gone as quickly as it came, but I watched him warily.

"I don't own you," Maximus said. "We're going to get you out of here. You are your own master now, Ariana."

I could feel the strength in his words, the conviction. I let go of the edge of my shirt and straightened my shoulders. This pack bond thing wasn't all bad. I could tell he meant what he said, that he really was getting me out. I tried to push it further, to see his intentions for me.

He gave me a haughty smile. "It doesn't work that way."

Startled, I retreated a step. "How does it work?"

"You can feel strong emotion from us, and I can communicate with you when I need to. But we can't read minds. Even I can't do that, though right now your emotions are very... open."

I crossed my arms over my chest, trying to hold in whatever he was seeing. I knew better than to show weakness to an opponent and let him exploit it.

"I'm going to bring my second-in-command down," Maximus said, his voice softening. "I know you don't trust me, and you have no reason to. But I'm not going to take advantage of you, Ariana. Not now, and not ever."

A moment later, an East Indian woman dropped into the pit beside us. Her long hair was held back in a low knot, and her brown eyes pooled with concern. The moment she was near, the intensity of her emotion made me step back. She held out a hand. "I'm Shira—the pack's second. We're going to take you home now, okay?"

Her tone was one used to calm a wild animal, which was slightly insulting and embarrassingly soothing. I nodded.

"Let's get her out of here," Maximus said. There were three exits to the pits. One led to the stands and was used only by my former master and the special guests he brought down to gawk at his prize killers.

Killers like me.

The fighters used the remaining doors on either ends of the pit. One led back to the cages and a bowl full of food. I didn't know where the other door led. I'd never lost a fight.

Maximus started towards that door, Shira close behind. Instinctually, I fell in behind them. But two steps later, my mind balked.

Shira gasped audibly, the heel of her hand pressing against her temple. She and Maximus both turned to me.

"You're going to have to teach her to put up some shields," Shira muttered to him. "If not for her sake, then for ours."

"I know that," Maximus snapped. His gaze held only patience for me, though.

"I'm not going out that way," I said. "That's the loser's door. I use the winner's door." My words sounded cold even to my ears, but damn it if he couldn't see past them, see the fear bubbling in my stomach. That was the door of the dead. The only living things that used that door were the pit crew dragging out the bodies. The pit crew were only a step above the fighters—those who owed the master but were not shapeshifters.

Shit. The pack could see that, too. Maximus was flashing it back to me, showing me what I showed him. I wanted them out of my head. My thoughts were the only thing I had that was truly my own. Even my body belonged to my master.

"We can use the other door," Maximus said quietly.

I caught a flicker of surprise from Shira, but she followed behind when he strode toward the tunnel leading to the cages. I fell in behind them, uncertainty coursing through me as we approached. I hadn't been to the cages as a human since I was a kid, since... The memory of my parents caught me by surprise and I stumbled. Maximus glanced over his shoulder at me, his jaw tight.

*Hold it together, Ari*, I told myself.

Seen from human eyes, the cages looked pathetically small. Just big enough for a dog to sleep in the dirt. Empty food and water bowls.

I swallowed, sick with anger and humiliation. This was a terrible idea. I shouldn't have taken them back this way.

"There are more," Maximus said, pulling up short.

"Of course there are more," I said. "People require entertainment like dogs require food."

I winced as I said the line that my master had said to me so many times.

Maximus's shoulders squared. "We're not dogs. We are wolves."

I didn't argue, though it made no difference to the master—or to me. I'd fought dogs, and the trick to winning was the same. Take out their front legs instead of going right for the throat.

"I'll have someone get the key to these and release the captives," Maximus said. "Let's get you out of here."

We passed the remaining cages and exited the building, stepping into a balmy night. Trees along the edge of the parking lot tossed in a gust of wind. I closed my eyes and inhaled, taking in the scent of fresh air that so rarely made it down to the cages under the stands.

My eyes snapped open. I hated fresh air. It was the scent of new arrivals being brought through this door and shoved into cages, usually screaming and pleading for mercy.

Shira grimaced at me. I couldn't help what she was seeing. Maybe she should learn to stay out of my head.

"It's the first thing I'll teach you," she said as we approached the car.

Maximus climbed in the driver's seat, and I didn't hesitate to open the back door and slide onto the leather seat. The only thing on my mind was getting the hell out of here as fast as possible. I could worry about where we were going later. It couldn't be worse than this.

"We're taking you to our home," Maximums said. "We prefer to live close. It helps with communication."

He spoke as we pulled out of the parking lot and headed north, out of the city. They lived an hour outside the city, he said, on a mountain. The pack owned the whole mountain, and he lead the pack. He said we were safe from the warlock, but I wasn't so sure. He wouldn't let me go so easily. I was bound to him—my parents had pledged service to him. He owned us. The idea of being free, of owning myself, was impossible to comprehend. But I knew one thing for sure. I wasn't going back without a fight. And so far, fighting me had not worked out so well for my opponents.

As promised, we pulled into Maximus's werewolf community an hour after leaving the city. Also as promised, Shira and Maximus went over the basics of how to keep them out of my head during the drive. I had pictured brick walls coming up around me, and relief showed in both of the wolves.

By the time they told me we were entering their territory, I was mentally and physically exhausted. The car climbed the low mountain, winding back and forth through a series of switchbacks. Through the trees to my right, I could just make out high bluffs shining white in the moonlight. Above them, scattered over the top of the mountain, were a handful of little houses and one big house at the top. A few minutes later, we pulled up in front of the large wooden lodge.

"Let's get you settled in for the night," Maximus

said, getting out of the car and stretching. The moonlight glimmered off his strong back, the muscles knotting under his bare skin.

"It is late," Shira said, yawning. "And I'm sure we've all had enough excitement for one day."

I balked at the thought of going into their house, but Maximus smiled and fed me a picture of a bed. I edged a step closer. Then he gave me more images—a spacious living room with the sun streaming through the window, a leather couch and a bookshelf, feet up on the coffee table and coffee steaming beside me...or him? I was still confused about how the bond worked, if I was seeing the past or the future. When I didn't rush into the house, he tempted me further with the image of a plate full of spaghetti. That did it.

I could at least eat here, and rest. Then, I'd figure out what they wanted.

Inside, Shira led me upstairs and showed me the bathroom and a bedroom. "You can wear my clothes until you get a few of your own," she said, opening her bureau for me. "Come downstairs when you're ready to eat."

I was ready to eat now, but the thought of the shower was enticing, and I was more than ready to get my body covered. I took a quick shower and pulled on the yoga pants and long-sleeved tee I'd chosen.

When I stepped out of the bathroom, the smell of food drew me straight downstairs and into the kitchen. Maximus turned from the stove, a plate in each hand.

He'd pulled on a plain white T-shirt with his dress pants, and for the first time, I noticed how handsome he was. His strong jawline and chiseled cheekbones were subtly highlighted by the dark shadow of stubble across his cheeks and chin. Bright hazel eyes met mine, a smile playing over his lips.

Damn it. Was he picking up on my admiration?

"I'll eat with you," he said, delivering the plates of spaghetti to the table. He sat opposite me and passed me a bowl of parmesan. I dug in without hesitation, famished after the fight and the long day without food that preceded it.

"Shira showed you the bedroom where you can sleep?" he asked.

I nodded, eating quickly without speaking. Sometimes, they gave us only enough food to whet our appetites before pulling it away, taunting us with the bowl that sat just out of reach.

"You're going to be safe here," Maximus said. "I can tell you're tired, so just eat and then you can sleep in the guest room. We'll talk more in the morning."

I was grateful for his understanding, even if he'd poked around in my mind to get there. After eating, I retreated to the room they'd left me and fell into an exhausted sleep immediately.

I woke after a few hours. I wasn't used to sleeping a whole night at a time. A lot of business took place at night with vampires coming and going, new residents arriving in the cages, and other commotion. Now that

I'd slept, my mind was clearer. I slipped from the big bed and listened. My wolf urged me to get out, to run. And she was right. I didn't know what these people wanted, but I knew for damn sure that their kindness wouldn't come without a price. Everyone wanted something. That was the way the world worked. If I wanted to eat, I had to fight. If I wanted to live, I had to win.

I tiptoed from the room, stopping in the hallway to listen. I could hear soft snores from down the hall. My heart pounding, I slipped silently down the stairs. All the while, I waited for an alarm or a guard to stop me. But none did. It was almost as if I were free to come and go as I pleased.

What if it could really be that simple?

I shook my head and started towards the woods, needing to put some distance between myself and these wolves with mysterious motives. What did they want from me? Was that what Maximus meant to tell me today when we talked?

As I stepped into the woods, a sense of familiarity washed over me. I'd played in the woods as a child, before the old warlock had died and passed us on to his son. He'd let me roam the woods and creeks like a wild animal, though I knew I must always return home. He'd been kind to us, but we never forgot that we belonged to him.

My wolf was even more comfortable in the woods than my human side. She strained to get out, but I was hesitant. I wasn't sure that I could control her, that I could choose this form at will. I had been forced into it by Maximus's command as alpha. But already the bonds were weakening. I could feel the tie with the pack loosening as I moved further away, deeper into the forest.

At last, I found a tangle of briars and vines where I could crawl under and rest. I'd never had a pack, and I didn't need one now. I'd survived more than they ever would, and I'd done it on my own. Out here, the trees provided protection and privacy. There were plenty of animals to hunt. My wolf would take care of me. She knew how to survive. And no one would demand payment for favors.

## 4

## ARIANA

When I awoke the next morning, I knew they were looking for me. Rays of warm sunlight peeked through the brambles, warning me of dawn. I yawned and stretched, only to feel the prick of briars at my ankles. I winced and retracted my feet, glaring at the surrounding foliage.

*Ariana.*

I looked around quickly before realizing Maximus spoke in my head again. I resisted an irritated groan and shimmied out from under the copse of shrubs. The same deep voice spoke my name again, and I quickly slammed up the brick walls Maximus and Shira had taught me to construct.

Though I could feel the concern of the pack, it was distant, like a whisper over my mind. I took a deep breath and straightened my clothes—or Shira's clothes. Smudges of dirt marred the once clean clothing, and for a second, I felt bad. It had been a long time since someone showed me kindness. And I'd already run away.

My heart lurched painfully, and I gripped the hem of my shirt. I knew I shouldn't feel guilty. I didn't know these people, and I couldn't trust them. The only people I'd ever been able to trust were gone. Dead. There was only me and my wolf.

As if on queue, my wolf strained forward, desperate to be free of the mental cage I'd shoved her into. I bit my lip. She showed me images of us running through the forest, one with the wind as we leapt over fallen trees and across streams. But though I wanted to trust my wolf, I didn't know if it'd be easy to return to my human form. I knew my wolf had kept me safe by taking over the last few years, but now that I'd gotten *me* back, I wasn't so ready to lose her again.

Taking a deep breath, I calmed my racing heart and pushed away the voices of the pack. I had to think. It had been so long since I'd had my head, I didn't know where to start. Though my wolf could protect me out here in the wild—provide me with food, safety, and comfort—did I want more than that? Something about Maximus and the others called to me, pulling on my soul to return to the lodge and be with my pack.

But was it *my* pack? Maximus had forced this bond on me, and that act in itself was certainly not going to make me trust him. Instead of sorting through my thoughts, I started walking away from pack territory. I instinctively knew I was heading away from it. As the voices in my head grew distant, my shoulders relaxed and I took in the crisp scent of morning air.

Through the trees, I spotted the same cliffs I'd admired on the drive in. As a child, I'd loved to climb. Trees. Rocks. Hills. Cliffs. If I could find anything that towered above me, I wanted to climb it.

That same, familiar sensation of wanting to be above the world itched in my bones, and I changed course toward the steep hills. Adrenaline wormed through my veins, and my pulse pounded in my ears.

Before I knew it, I was racing through the trees, my wolf howling inside me. She wanted to be free to run with me, and eventually I would let her. I knew I couldn't keep her at bay forever, but for now, I needed to remember what it was like to be human.

I reached the bottom of the cliff in a small clearing. Trees ascended from the top of it, barely visible from this angle. I inspected the rocky face for handholds, of which there were many. It had to be thirty feet high, not a bad climb for my first one in ten years.

My fingers tapped my thighs as I created a clear path from bottom to top in my mind. Once I had it, I went to the wall, trailing my fingers across the rough surface before digging my hands around the first set of holds just above my head.

Excitement rocketed through me, stealing my breath as I heaved myself up once, then twice. Soon, I was two feet above the ground. Then five. Then ten.

My muscles shook with strain, and sweat trickled down my back. It was harder than I remembered. Still, my excitement wouldn't be tamed as I edged upward, one hold at a time.

Ten feet from the from the top, I jammed my fingers into a crevice and held tight. I was just above the trees now, and the forest stretched out around me.

I dug my toes into a small nook and pushed. The stone slipped beneath my foot, grinding against the cliff before tumbling to the forest floor. My heart lurched and I clung to the cliff face, grappling for another toe hold. I expected something else to shift and send me to my death, but nothing did.

It took me several long minutes and several deep breath to regain my composure. When I finally stopped shaking, I turned my attention back to the wall and pushed myself up once again.

A sudden whoosh overhead had me leaning back. *What now?*

The trees shook with a violent wind and a beast like I'd never seen before shot over the edge of the cliff, scaled wings splayed on either side of its massive form. A cry of shock escaped my throat as it flapped its wings and the current caught me off guard. I dug my toes and fingers into my holds, but the current was too strong. A gasp tumbled from my lips as I was yanked right off the side of the cliff.

My heart raced as I desperately threw out a plea for help to anyone that might be able to save me. I was too high up, and I'd break every bone in my body if I hit the ground. Time seemed to slow as I twisted in mid-air. The rocky ground below was coming up way too fast.

I was going to die.

I'd survived the pits, Dante, the death of my parents, and torture for years, only to die from falling off a damn cliff.

The irony wasn't lost on me, and I would have laughed if I had any breath in my lungs. I closed my eyes, accepting my fate.

Instead of rocky ground, something warm caught me, and my eyes flashed open. A set of chiselled arms held me to a bare chest, one arm hooked around my back, the other beneath my legs. My cheek pressed against the man's shoulder, and heat flamed through my cheeks.

"Hang on tight," he said.

I glanced up, but being pressed so closely, I could only make out dark hair and gorgeous mocha skin. His angular jaw was covered in dark stubble, and I swore I saw a flash of green eyes. He squeezed me tighter, and I lost sight of his eyes, but over his shoulder, red wings beat the air.

I gasped. "What are you?"

I'd read fairytales as a child—damsels trapped in towers, knights sneaking into the dens of dragons seeking glory. It wasn't possible, and yet, here he was. A man with dragon wings.

Wait. Had it been him who flew overhead? My eyebrows furrowed and flames of anger burned inside my belly. He'd nearly *killed* me!

The man chuckled, and his lips twitched in a smile. He didn't respond, and that only fanned my fire.

"Put me down!" I growled. My wolf, who'd seemed stunned until this moment, growled inside me, but it wasn't the fury I expected of the beast that had protected me all my life. Instead, her growl was akin to a cat's purr.

*Mine*, she whispered.

What? Mine?! Was she fucking kidding me?

"If I put you down right now, you'll plummet to your death," the dragon man said. There was a slight edge of mockery in his tone that made me narrow my eyes. When I didn't answer, he laughed. "You're a wolf aren't you? One of Maximus's?"

My eyes widened. "Where are you taking me?"

"Back to your pack."

Damn. I'd nearly been free of them, and now he was taking me back. "Could you take me somewhere else?"

His grip stiffened, and I sensed his confusion as much as I felt my own. He didn't say a word, and over the edge of the trees, a large wooden lodge came into view. Several wolves were in the yard with a couple of humans.

The dragon man swooped through the air, angling down toward the front of the house. I ground my teeth and prepared to spring from his grip the moment we landed.

Even as the rest of me coiled for action, my wolf pressed against my mind, urging me to stay in this stranger's warm, muscled, incredibly strong…

I stopped her right there. There was no time for these thoughts. I had to get out of there before someone scented me.

Our descent slowed, and the dragon man angled his wings overhead, scooping the air until he touched down.

Before I could leap away, he set me on my feet, making sure I was steady before he released my elbow and stepped back.

The moment I saw his gorgeous face, all thoughts of fleeing temporarily evaporated. My eyes widened as I took in his face, like a greek god, but East Indian like Shira.

Our eyes met, and his widened. His lips parted in a silent gasp.

"The Silver Shifter," he whispered.

*The what?* My forehead wrinkled in confusion. His hands went to my shoulders, squeezing lightly.

"He's found you." His voice was filled with such awe that my entire body began to heat. The feeling was unfamiliar, and I quickly stepped away. I needed some space to get my head on straight and figure out what the hell was going on.

"Ariana!" Maximus called from the front door.

Shit.

I looked over my shoulder at the alpha making his way across the driveway. His shoulders relaxed, and his eyes lit up before narrowing on the man who'd saved me.

"Cash," Maximus growled.

The dragon man stiffened, his nostrils flaring. The awe drained from his face as it twisted in anger. "Maximus." Cash's fists clenched and a growl rumbled from his chest, deeper than I'd ever heard from a shifter. "What is the meaning of this?"

Maximus slid an arm around me and pulled me away from Cash, holding me protectively against his strong body. I bit my tongue on a growl and shot him a glare, but Maximus and Cash were in the middle of their own stare down.

"What are you doing here?" Maximus asked, ignoring Cash's question.

"You dare to question me when you're harboring the Silver Shifter without even informing the clans?"

I looked between the two, my irritation suddenly replaced with confusion. What were they talking about? What on earth was the Silver Shifter, and how did it relate to me?

Maximus snarled. "We only found her yesterday. She's hardly had time to adjust yet."

She? So *I* was this mysterious Silver Shifter that had Cash so upset.

"You should have called the moment you found

her. You know we've all been searching for twenty years." Cash's green eyes flashed and his pupils slit like a cat's.

My wolf whined inside. She was just as confused as me.

"I was going to." Maximus hesitated, his tensed shoulders lowering slightly. "But there were unforeseen circumstances."

Cash stilled. His pupils returned to normal. "What kind of circumstances?"

They glanced at me before exchanging a long look. Maximus finally let out a sigh of defeat. "I'll explain... when we're alone."

Again, they both looked at me, and I knew they were going to keep me out of this very important conversation.

# 5
## ARIANA

"The others will want to know about this," Cash said. "And they deserve to know. You should have told us the moment she was in your custody."

I bristled at his words. I was in Maximus's custody? Was that what this was? He'd told me I was bonded with his pack temporarily. Not that I was a prisoner in his house.

"What the hell is going on?" I demanded. I'd had enough of being spoken about like I wasn't there. I'd put up with that in wolf form because I'd had no choice. But now I had my thoughts back under my control—and my tongue.

Maximus sighed and ran a hand through his glossy chestnut hair. "Ariana, why don't you go inside and get something to eat. Shira will get you something clean to wear as well."

"It's their right to know," Cash growled at Maximus, his wings snapping against the air in irritation. "You have to tell them, Maximus. Better yet, I will. You seem to have your hands full here."

"Fine," Maximus said, his shoulders slumping. "Tell them to come tomorrow. I'd hoped she'd have more time to adjust, but I suppose it can't be helped."

"Damn right," Cash said. "I'll change course and deliver the news now." His eyes moved to me, drinking me in. "I'll see you tomorrow, Ariana."

My name sounded exotic on his lips, and I couldn't help the warm shiver that went through my body when his eyes lingered on mine for just a beat. He crouched slightly and then shot upwards into the air. He began to beat his wings, and the current through the air sent me reeling backwards.

Maximus leapt forward and caught me, his strong arm supporting my back.

"I'm okay," I said, but I let him hold onto me as I watched Cash streak across the sky. I'd just met a freaking dragon!

"Let's get inside," Maximus said. "Shira's waiting for you."

"Want to explain to me what's going on?" I asked. "What's all this Silver Shifter talk? I mean, obviously my hair is silver, but you act like it's a big deal."

"It is a big deal," Maximus said, looking weary. "And so is your safety."

"Which is why you forced me into your pack?" I

asked. "That's why I'm a prisoner here, just like I was in the pits?"

"No. It's not like that," Maximus said. "I would never mistreat a member of my own pack."

"Yeah, well, that pack nonsense is wearing off real quick," I said. "So what happens when I'm not a member of your pack?"

A pained expression crossed his face. "I know you have no reason to trust me, but I would never hurt you, Ariana. Never."

He was right that I had no reason to trust him, and yet, I could tell through the bond that he had no ill will toward me. But he had to want something, and his reluctance to answer my questions only raised my suspicions.

I had been hungry for a long time, though. I couldn't remember a time when the gnawing pain wasn't a constant companion. So I followed Maximus inside when he walked up the steps and into the lodge. As promised, Shira had laid the table with food —quiche, fresh fruit, wheat toast, a pitcher of orange juice, and a carafe of coffee.

"Let's eat," Maximus said, taking a seat at the head of the table.

"Anything else you want?" Shira asked.

At first I thought she was talking to Maximus, her alpha. But then I realized she was staring right at me, waiting for my answer. I started to say no— being picky meant being hungry. Before I could, a memory from childhood rose unbidden to my mind.

"Do you have chocolate milk?" I asked.

"I'm afraid we don't," she said. "I can get some next time we go into town."

"Don't worry about it," I said, suddenly self-conscious at their eyes on me.

"I'll make you some," Maximus said, pushing back from the table.

"It's okay, really," I said.

"Just let him make it," Shira said. She patted my hand as Maximus took some chocolate syrup from the refrigerator. She lowered her voice to a whisper. "Trust me, he'll order you around plenty. On the rare occasions he wants to be of service, enjoy it."

"I heard that," Maximus said, his back to us as he poured milk into the glass with the chocolate.

Shira rolled her eyes and offered me a smile before he returned to the table. "For our guest," he said, bowing gallantly and handing me the chocolate milk.

I couldn't help but smile. "Thank you," I said, taking a sip. The sweetness of chocolate burst on my tongue and I had to suppress a moan. "I haven't had this since I was a kid."

"Me, neither," Maximus said, pouring himself some coffee. "Adults don't usually drink chocolate milk."

I decided right then that I'd be drinking it every day.

"Now, let's get some things straight," Maximus said, squaring his shoulders. "Ariana, you can't go running off like you did. It's not safe out there, as you now know. What if Cash hadn't been there to stop your fall?"

I jerked in my seat. For a moment, I questioned how he knew I'd fallen in the first place, but then my desperate mental plea came to mind. Even so, angry heat rose inside of me.

"If Cash hadn't been there, I wouldn't have fallen," I shot back, not bothering to hide my irritation.

"I'm trying to protect you," Maximus growled. "Please stop being so stubborn and do as I ask, while I'm still asking. You've gotten us into enough trouble today."

My wolf stirred. "You mean I got *you* into trouble."

"Yes," he said. "And yourself. I'm the pack's leader. I need to know where my members are and that they're safe. I can't have you wandering around and falling off cliffs."

My wolf growled at that. "So I'm not free to take a walk? I might as well be back in the pits."

Maximus's eyes flashed with anger. "That's not something to joke about."

"You think I don't know that?" Now my wolf was straining to break free, to have at this man who was upsetting me. Pushing her back, I grabbed my chocolate milk and chugged the whole thing, refusing to let his anger intimidate me. I'd been in a cage most of my life, and before that, even when I was "free," I'd been the property of a warlock. Now, I'd been promised freedom for the first time in my life, and I wasn't about to give it up this easily. I slammed my glass down and glared at him.

"You're acting like a child," Maximus said through clenched teeth.

"I was born into the service of that warlock, but if you don't have paperwork to prove it, then I don't belong to you."

"You don't belong to me," Maximus said stiffly. I could tell he was barely controlling his anger to speak to me in an even tone. "But you *should* belong to this pack. Wolves need protection, and I can protect you."

"No," I said. "I'm done being owned and controlled. If you want me to stay, I'll stay for now, but I need to be able to do what I want—to come and go when I want. And I'm not taking the bond."

"Bullshit," Maximus burst out, his fist slamming against the table. "I can't protect you if I don't know where you are."

"I don't need your protection," I said, my hands clenching into fists. The wolf inside me roared to come out and join the fight. "And I won't be forced into your pack and have you listening in on my every thought."

"I can show you—" Shira started, but I cut her off.

"I don't care," I said, jumping to my feet. "I'm not your pet, and I'm not your property. I belong to myself now. Myself and my wolf."

I couldn't hold the howl inside me any longer. Stumbling back from the table, I let it out as pain gripped my body. Relief washed over me as I stopped fighting my other half and let her out.

I had to tear at the clothes on my body, and by the time I'd ripped them off with my wolf teeth, Maximus had undressed and shifted, too. He lowered his head and drew his lips back, his nose wrinkling as he bared his teeth and growled.

Without having been raised in a pack, I was surprised at how instinctually my wolf interpreted his warning snarl. He was telling me to straighten up or he'd make me. And I wasn't about to let him.

I lunged for him, going right for his front legs. Maximus's head slammed into mine, knocking me off course, and he snapped loudly. I was within reach, and he could have bitten me, but instead, he slammed his shoulder into me. My body went flying, crashing to the floor. As I rolled over, ready to spring to my feet, Maximus leapt onto me, pinning me down.

He growled low in his throat, his eyes locking on mine.

*Obey your alpha.*

His words crashed into my head, so intense I was forced to drop my gaze. A hideously pitiful whine escaped my wolf throat. Maximus lowered his head and licked my cheek. Instead of submitting further, I used his vulnerable moment to take him by surprise. I lunged at him, sinking my teeth into the side of his neck.

With a howl of pain, he wrenched free. Blood splattered across my face and the floor. Somewhere in the back of my mind, I heard the fading sound of the pack, but it didn't register. I was in fight mode now, like I'd been in the pits. I'd drawn blood, and my only job now was to finish him off.

Lunging again, I went for his throat. Maximus leapt off me, and I was back on my feet in seconds. He sprang aside when I went for his legs, and before I could turn and go back in, something heavy crashed onto my back. I went rolling again, and this time, two wolves pinned me while Maximus stood over me, his tail held high, like the bastard was proud of having me subdued in this humiliating way.

Even worse, a second later, Shira circled around behind me and pulled a muzzle over my snout, pinning my mouth shut. I roared in rage inside the thing, straining every muscle to break free.

Maximus swiftly transformed back into human form, and together with Shira and two others I didn't know, he hauled me through a door at the side of the kitchen. A dark opening gaped before me, smelling like dank dirt and mildew. I tried to brace my legs against the door, but they forced me through, carrying me down a set of stairs.

No, no, no...this couldn't be happening. No more cages.

"Then don't act like an animal," Maximus said gruffly.

My rage had not diminished, but I couldn't get free in my wolf form. In an effort to surprise them, I forced back my wolf side and shifted into human form. I regretted it the instant I felt their hands on my bare skin.

"Let me go, you sick bastards!" I screamed.

"Put her in there until she calms down," Maximus said, nodding at one of three large silver cages.

But no matter how pretty they were, no matter how the silver bars gleamed, they were still cages. Prisons like the ones I'd lived in for so long.

They pushed me inside, and I flew at the bars, screaming and yanking on them even as I heard the lock click into place. Maximus stood looking at me with a haughty, superior expression even as he held his shirt against his bleeding neck. He'd even taken the time to put his pants on while the others forced me into submission. Blood bloomed on the fabric he held to his wound, but I was too angry to care that I'd bitten the man who had shared his house with me and showed me such generosity. Underneath it all, he was like all the others in my life who had wanted to control me, own me, cage me.

"You won't get away with this," I snarled at him. "I'll fucking kill you next time."

"I'm not your owner, but I am your alpha," he said coolly, arching one eyebrow. "You can cool down in there, as any of our pack members must when they get out of control. When you're in your right mind, I'll be ready to talk to you."

The others rushed to follow when he turned and walked away, his head held high.

# 6
## OWEN

The Silver Shifter was found. Excitement thrummed inside me as I drove my pickup truck into wolf territory. The scent of the beasts hit me and a breath hissed between my teeth. It wasn't often shifters crossed into one another's territory. In fact, it was forbidden unless given express permission or there was an emergency. So when Cash had arrived in bear territory last night, I knew something was up.

The same elation his words had given me then filled me now. Maximus had found the Silver Shifter. She was a wolf and apparently had a habit of falling off cliffs. I smiled at the thought of the Silver Shifter being clumsy. I'd never lived through the reign of another, but Cash had. His mother had been the last Silver Shifter.

I was glad to be the alpha of the bears in the time

when a legendary Silver Shifter had been found. It was an exciting time. I wondered what gift she would have, how she would bring harmony to our clans. The fact that she was supposedly the last Silver Shifter ever made it even more of an honor to meet and negotiate with her.

The trees lining the long dirt driveway widened to circle an enormous clearing with Maximus's lodge at the center. If I wasn't a part of the supernatural world, I might have thought it was just a ski lodge closed for the season, but the strong scent of wolves made it clear who owned the surrounding area.

A dark blue Jeep was parked beside a silver Lincoln next to the entrance of the lodge. My eyebrows shot up as I inspected the sleek curves. I'd never been one for luxury cars, but damn, I think this was the first time I'd ever been jealous of Cash. That was one nice car.

I pulled in next to the others, ripping the e-brake and silencing the hum of my truck before climbing out. For a pack that just found their Silver Shifter after years of searching, the lodge was awfully quiet. I'd expected some sort of grand celebration or at least a barbeque. Crickets chirped in the heat of the sun, and birds fluttered from the treetops. Nothing else moved.

Confusion furrowed my brow as I approached the front door. Seriously, what was going on? Where was everyone?

I took one last look around before knocking, three

swift raps on the door. The door creaked open, and the pack's second-in-command stood in the doorway.

"Owen," Shira said.

"Shira." I furrowed my brow at her curt nod. Normally, Shira was all smiles and wore some pretty intensely colored clothes. But today, her lips curved into a frown, and she worried the edge of her gray blouse.

"Come in." She stepped aside to let me through and closed the door behind me.

Cash stood from the leather sofa in the living room. His dark gaze met mine, and I knew immediately something was wrong.

"What's going on?" I asked. I tried to keep my tone light, more like a joke, but it fell flat.

Cash grimaced. "I'm not sure yet." He looked around the living room, then at the door to the kitchen and the stairs to the second floor. He was looking for something or someone. The Silver Shifter?

"So, where is she?"

"Ariana," Cash said.

It was a pretty name for what I was sure was a pretty girl. The Silver Shifters were known for their ethereal beauty. I tested out her name. "Ariana."

Cash met my eyes, and his jaw hardened. He didn't say anything as Maximus descended the stairs to join us.

Maximus greeted us curtly, wearing the same surly look as Cash, but with the worried brow of Shira.

"Will someone tell me what's going on already?" My hands fisted at my sides. Irritation shot through me. I'd been so excited to come and meet the new Silver Shifter. I'd heard so many things about what she might be like and the peace she would bring. After the Silver Dragon was assassinated, the clans had fallen back to their old ways. We all distrusted one another, and with no idea who'd ended the life of the last Silver Shifter, we'd never had a reason to find peace when any one of us could be the killer.

"I'll explain once Jett arrives." Maximus avoided both of our gazes, instead staring at the door to the basement.

"Jett's always late," Cash said. I wasn't sure if it was a complaint or just an observation.

A growl interrupted the quiet, emanating from the door Maximus stared at. My heart lurched with the realization a shifter was down there. "Maximus," I said. "What are you keeping down there?"

Maximus shot me a look, and my irritation turned to outrage.

*This better not be what I think it is.*

I stormed over to the door and yanked it open.

The growling grew louder, and the distinct scent of an angry werewolf flew up my nostrils. I looked back in time to see realization cross Cash's face, too. Maximus looked between us and the door. At least he had the decency to look guilty.

"It's where we keep werewolves who break laws,"

he said quickly. "It's just a holding cell for them to cool down. A time out."

I turned back to the darkness of the stairs and flicked on the overhead light before descending to a landing and turning left to finish the rest of the steps to the basement floor.

Snarls ripped through the quiet, and claws grated the cement floor. I squinted through the dim light, looking for the source of the sound. Only faint daylight streamed through two tiny basement windows on the edge of the basement. The rest was left in shadow.

The tread of boots and the light click of dress shoes told me Cash and Maximus followed.

"You don't understand what she came from," Max said.

Finally, I spied the light switch and flicked it on. Blinding fluorescent light sent sparks of white across my vision. I blinked to clear them. Shadows merged into shapes and left me staring at a row of cages lining the back wall. Each had silver bars, unbreakable to werewolves. Only one cell was occupied by a thin silver wolf with her head lowered and her lips pulled back, baring her teeth in a snarl.

The wolf snapped at the bars before pulling back and pacing the cell.

It took me a moment to collect my thoughts and process what I was seeing. A wolf with silver pelt, locked inside a cage.

"Ariana?" I whispered.

The wolf paused, her ears swivelling. Her growling ceased.

"What the hell were you thinking?" Cash snapped at Maximus.

The two alphas stood side by side next to the stairs. Cash motioned at the cage, embers of rage kindling in his eye just like the ones in my belly.

"You don't understand," Maximus said again.

"No, we don't!" I bellowed. "So why don't you explain to us why you'd lock the *Silver Shifter* in a cage?"

Ariana tilted her head as she considered us. Gone was the fierce animal that prowled the cell. She was beautiful but small, her ribs nearly visible on her thin haunches.

"How long has she been down here?" I demanded.

"Only the night," Maximus said.

Cash laid a hand on my arm. "He's telling the truth. I saw her just yesterday, remember?"

His words calmed my bear, whose instincts flared inside my head, snapping at me to release Ariana *now*.

"Still," I insisted. I couldn't believe the wolves were keeping her down there. They should be worshipping the ground she walked on. I took a step toward the cage. "You can't keep her in there."

"I had to do this, Owen," Maximus said.

"Like hell!" I stormed forward, and in one swift yank, tore the lock from the front of the cage.

Ariana's silver gaze widened as she looked between me and the lock I'd tossed to the floor. I pulled the cage bars back just as Maximus yelled for me to stop. It was too late. The gate was already open before I saw the murder in Ariana's eyes.

## 7
## ARIANA

I bolted out of the cage with one thought on my mind—freedom.

"Ariana, stop!" Maximus yelled, but I wasn't about to obey him. Not after he'd stuck me in a cage just like Dante. Fuck that shit. I was so out of there.

I lunged past the man they'd called Owen, ignoring Cash and Maximus. Scrambling up the stairs, I charged for the open door. I would never be put in a cage again. If I had to die to make that vow come true, so be it. They'd have to take me down fighting.

When I reached the top of the stairs, I leapt, sailing through the opening.

A wall of muscle met me in midair, and I thudded to the floor. In seconds I was back on my feet, going straight for the man's groin. That always took down a human. A fist slammed straight into my mouth, crushing into the back of my throat. Gagging, I tried to pull back, but he grabbed the skin at the back of my neck with his free hand, maneuvering me. I couldn't breathe, and I couldn't bite down because his fist was in my throat. Panic swelled inside me at my helpless position.

"So nice of you to finally join us, Jett," Maximus said behind me. "Late, as usual."

"Ain't this some shit," Jett drawled in a slow, slight southern accent. "I thought I was coming for a civil discussion. If you don't change my mind in a hurry, I'm going to assume this is an ambush."

"It's not an ambush," Maximus growled. "That's her. So get your fist out of her throat before you kill her."

The man holding me straddled by back, wrapping his arm around my neck in warning before removing his hand. A piteous whimper escaped my throat, though inside, it was more like a roar of rage. I stood catching my breath, my muscles trembling.

"You've got to be kidding me," my attacker said. He started laughing then, hooting and slapping his knee as he held me in a headlock. "Your Silver Shifter mate is feral. That's the funniest thing I've heard all year."

"I'm glad you're amused," Maximus said stiffly. "Now bring her back downstairs."

At that, I began to struggle. The bond he'd forced on me was almost completely gone, but I could feel a command worming through what was left of it. He wanted me to shift back to human form. *Yeah, right.* I had no intention of making this easy for them.

"I won't put you in a cage," Maximus said when they reached the bottom of the stairs. He didn't bother with the telepathic shit this time, just said it out loud. "Stop attacking us for a minute, and we can help you understand what's going on."

"You sure you want me to let her go?" asked Jett. "I know how to fight a dog. I've had a few fights with y'all before. But you might want to shift first."

"We're not dogs," Maximus snapped.

"It's your neck," the guy said, releasing his choke hold on me.

I darted away, crossing the room to the far wall, where I spun to face them. This time, they'd closed the basement door behind them, which meant that even if I could make it past them again, I'd have to shift to human form to open it. And if I couldn't fight them off as a wolf, I sure as hell couldn't do it as a human.

"Ariana, you're welcome to join us when you're ready," Maximus said. "We'd be happy to have you as part of this discussion. I'll have Shira bring you some clothes."

I bared my teeth and growled.

Maximus turned to the others. "She was in the pits in the city," he said. "Fighting other shifters. I don't know how long she's been there."

"Nobody lasts long in that place," Owen said, his brow furrowed with concern as he studied me.

"I know," Maximus said, shaking his head.

As my wolf calmed, human thoughts crept in again. Thoughts that did not fit into an escape plan at all. The four of them stood watching me, lined up with their arms crossed. My human side wanted to get out, to be with them. To see them as a human would see them.

My wolf side... she had something else on her mind, too. Less coherent, but no less confusing.

*Mine, mine, mine, mine*, echoed through her head like a chant. My wolf wanted to taste their blood, to claim them as her own. But which one?

Wolves had one mate. And since I was a wolf, that meant only Maximus could be my mate, as much as I despised the thought. Sure, he looked good standing there with the others, his dark hair swept back from his forehead, those angular cheekbones and strong jaw set as he looked at me. But the guy was a hard-ass control freak, and that didn't go over well with me.

The others couldn't be my mates. Wolves didn't mate with dragon men or whatever the others were.

But they looked so good I was nearly salivating. I wanted to bite them. To make them mine. All of them, not just Maximus. The new guy, Jett, stood a step apart from the others, his stance relaxed and easy. His brown skin had a slight sheen like silk, his bald head gleaming in the overhead light. A broad grin stretched across his face as if delighted by this turn of events.

Next to him, Cash stood with his wings folded

behind him, watching me with slight amusement, a smirk on his fine lips, his dark curls spilling over his forehead. Owen was a big, burly man with a barrel chest straining against his flannel shirt and sturdy, tree-trunk thighs. His blond hair was pulled back in a ponytail, his beard neatly trimmed.

My wolf must be a greedy bitch, because she wanted him, too. And the guy who had stuck his fist down her throat.

*Mine mine mine mine...*

Shira slipped through the door and trotted down the stairs, delivering a set of folded clothes to Maximus.

"Let me know if you need anything else," she said.

"I will," Maximus said.

Shira turned and disappeared up the stairs again. I eyed the door, but I wasn't crazy enough to make a run for it again. Last time, I'd taken them by surprise. I wouldn't have that advantage again.

"Looks like you've got a little problem on your hands," Jett said. "I'm going to enjoy watching you try to fix this, Maximus."

"Like it or not, this is not just my problem," Maximus said. "We all need the Silver Shifter."

"What are you going to do about her?" Cash asked. "Stick her back in that cage?"

I snarled, taking satisfaction in watching all the men jump a little.

"You can't put her in a cage," Owen said. "You saw how she reacted."

I decided he was my favorite.

*It doesn't matter, wolfie*, I tried to reason with myself. *Your mate has to be a wolf.*

"If she's too stubborn to reason with us, maybe that's where she belongs," Maximus said.

But does it have to be *him*?

"If she's been in a cage for a long time, putting her back there is not going to help," Owen said, his voice a low rumble. "It's no wonder she's pissed. You're treating her like you're her master, not her mate."

Maximus scowled. "Got any better ideas?"

"She needs time to adjust to all of this," Owen said.

I bristled a little. Even though he was being kind, I was tired of people deciding what I needed.

"We don't have time," Cash said. "It's a miracle the clans haven't declared all-out war by now."

"You going to tell her to get her shit together?" Jett asked, still grinning his fool head off. "I want to be around to see that."

"We need to be in agreement," Maximus said. "We've got to decide what to do about her *today*. You're right, Owen. She doesn't belong to me. She's my mate, though, so she stays here."

"You can have her," Jett said, holding up both hands. "I don't need more crazy in my life."

"She's not crazy," Owen said. "She's broken."

"And she'll stay here until she's healed," Maximus said matter-of-factly.

Okay, that was it. I'd had it with all of them. I shifted back into my human form with words already rolling off my tongue. "Stop talking about me like I'm not even here," I snapped. "I don't need any of you deciding where to keep me. In fact, if it weren't for your bossy asses, I'd be out in the forest and off your hands."

"Whoa," Owen said, his mouth falling open as he ogled me.

I was too mad to be embarrassed. "And stop acting like I'm too delicate to handle myself. I am neither crazy nor broken."

"She graces us with her presence at last," Jett said with a smirk.

"Always a pleasure," Maximus said dryly.

"I'm right here," I said, throwing my arms up and resisting the urge to stamp my foot.

"Yes, you are," Cash said, obviously enjoying my human form more than I was.

I snatched the clothes from Maximus's hand and pulled the T-shirt over my head. I tugged on the jeans without bothering to pull on the underwear provided. Now that I was dressed, I was even more aware of how naked I'd been. In front of all of them. Cash was staring at me like a cat eyeing a bowl of milk. I gulped, hugging myself.

"Ready to talk like a civilized human being?" Maximus asked.

"I am a civilized human being."

"Then act like one."

God, he was insufferable. And so freaking gorgeous. Even as a human, without my instinctual wolf side drooling over him, I couldn't help but be drawn in by those hazel eyes. He'd been kind to me, even if he had stuck me in a damn cage.

*Stop excusing what he did just because he's hot*, I scolded myself. Maybe my human hormones were going nuts to make up for lost time. I'd been a wolf for so long that maybe my human hormones were choosing now to flood my body.

*That doesn't explain my wolf calling them all her mates...*

"Can we go upstairs and get out of this cave?" Jett said. "Owen might be a bear, but panthers don't live in dens."

"You're a panther?" I asked, turning to Jett as Maximus started up the stairs.

"Yeah," Jett said, giving me an incredulous look. "And you're supposedly our savior."

"I'm getting really tired of people telling me what I am."

"No one's trying to tell you that," Owen said, his big hand falling gently on my lower back as he ushered me ahead of him towards the steps.

"Then maybe you should start by explaining what all of this is about."

"That's what we're trying to do," Maximus said as I stepped through the doorway into the kitchen. "If you'd calm down and stop running long enough to hear us out."

"Fine," I said, planting my hands on my hips and turning to face them. "Explain."

"You're the Silver Shifter," Maximus said. "Do you know what that is?"

"Does it look like I know what that is?"

"Let's all sit down and talk about this," Owen said in that low, rumbling voice. It sent an involuntary tremor through me, like he was an earthquake brewing deep below the surface of my conscience. I had a feeling that Earthquake Owen could shake up my life in ways I could only imagine.

We took our seats around the table. As my eyes moved from one man to the next, a second of hesitation gripped me. What if the truth was worse than the life I'd already known?

My anxiety was quickly overpowered by my need to know. I couldn't imagine a life worse than the mindless survival of my past. If these four beautiful men held the key to a different future, I was ready.

"Okay," I said, folding my hands on the table in front of me. "Tell me everything."

## 8
## ARIANA

"The Silver Shifter is a being born every hundred years," Cash began.

I was surprised Maximus hadn't started, but instead he went to the fridge and then a cupboard. With his large shoulders in the way, I couldn't tell what he was doing.

"Normally, you'd be born inside one of the clans. We'd know who you were from the second you were born," Cash continued. He raised his eyebrows meaningfully.

I snapped my attention away from whatever Maximus was up to and looked back at the Indian man in front of me. "Why wasn't I born inside the clans then?"

A pang of uncertainty gripped my heart. What would it have been like to grow up as part of a pack? Would I have had friends? Would my family still be alive? My eyebrows furrowed as I tried to imagine a life in which I had never been owned. I wasn't sure what that was like. In one way or another, someone was always telling me what to do, where to go, what I could and couldn't do. Even before Dante's father had died, we'd still had to adhere to a strict schedule with specific playtime outdoors, mealtimes, and bedtimes.

Did packs run the same way?

"The last of your kind, the Silver Dragon, had a rare power," Cash said. "She was an oracle. She predicted a lot about her successor."

"Me?"

Owen nodded as Cash went on. "She prophesied you would be born outside the clans, that you'd be found in your twenties, and your transition to the clans would be...difficult."

*Did she also predict I'd be locked in more damn cages the second I was found?*

I barely held back the snarky comment, biting down on my tongue before I made things worse.

"All Silver Shifters have a unique ability," Jett added, almost as if an afterthought. His gaze trailed over my face and down my baggy t-shirt, making my cheeks heat. "I'm sure we'll find out what yours is eventually."

"Okay," I said. I wasn't sure what else to say or what to make of this.

"Here." Maximus appeared at my side suddenly,

and I jumped like a skittish rabbit. He placed a tall glass of brown liquid in front of me.

"Chocolate milk?" I reached for it, licking my lips. I could already taste the sweet, glorious chocolate.

Maximus nodded curtly and took a seat beside me. He laid an arm across the back of my chair and didn't meet my eyes, even as I inspected his face for far longer than was appropriate.

While my wolf hummed her approval, unease twisted my gut. What did he want in return for this kindness?

"So..." Owen's voice cut through the awkward silence.

I forced my gaze away from Maximus and wrapped my fingers around the cool glass. No matter how suspicious the gesture was, I couldn't resist the offering.

"Do you know anything about the New York Clans?" Owen asked. His face was kind and open. He didn't sneer like Jett or smirk like Cash. It was much easier to relax under his calm blue gaze, so I focused on him while I sipped my drink.

"Nothing," I mumbled between sips.

"Well, there are four clans, as you might have guessed." Owen glanced at the other alphas. Jett inspected his nails like he was too good for this conversation while Maximus looked out the window. Only Cash seemed to be paying attention. "There are wolves, dragons, bears, and panthers."

He gestured at them each in turn, though I'd already guessed from process of elimination that Owen had to be the bear. It suited him. He was tall and broad, the largest of the four men.

"The clans have been at war on and off for as long as anyone can remember. At some point, the Silver Shifter was born. Each time the female being appeared, the warring stopped until she died. Each one has brought some sense of peace to the clans. She usually travels between them or holds meetings with the alphas. She acts kind of like a mediator for shifter business."

"A mediator?" I raised my eyebrows.

"Yes," Cash said. "The Silver Dragon was particularly good at this. She installed a few long term solutions that have kept us all in check…. So far." He shot a loaded glance at Maximus, but the wolf alpha said nothing.

"What happened to her?" I asked.

No one answered right away. Cash avoided my gaze.

"She was killed," Jett said. For once, a sneer didn't grace his face.

I froze. "Murdered?"

They all nodded. The air in the room felt suddenly thick, heavy on my shoulders and sticky on my skin. They expected me to take up the mantle of a murdered prophet? I didn't have any special skills besides, ironically, killing. I was particularly good at that.

"Who killed her?" I asked.

"No one knows," Cash said. His deep voice was laced with regret.

Each of them regarded each other with distrust. It seemed I'd opened an old wound. The alphas looked ready to lunge at the other's throats.

"You want me to replace her?" I had to ask.

Maximus shot me a surprised look. His eyebrows furrowed and he frowned. "No. Each Silver Shifter is her own person and has her own way of handling things."

"But I'll be expected to...what? Broker peace between all of you?"

"That's the simplest way of putting it." Cash sighed and ran a hand through his curly black hair.

I didn't know if I was up for that. I didn't know anything about their world or why they were fighting. There was something they weren't telling me even still. I could feel it.

"What else?" I asked tentatively.

"What else?" Jett scoffed. "This shit ain't enough for you?"

"What aren't you saying?" I snapped, narrowing my eyes at the panther alpha.

He grinned, flashing a dazzling set of teeth, but didn't say anything more. I looked at the others, but they were all remaining tight-lipped.

"If you want me to be your damn Silver Shifter, someone better talk right now."

Owen sighed. "The oracle... She had one last prophecy you should know about."

"Okay." My heart raced with anticipation. "What is it?"

Owen glanced at the others as if asking for permission. When he received a couple shrugs, he finally met my gaze again. "The Silver Dragon's last prediction was that you would be the uniter of clans and the *last* Silver Shifter."

My eyes widened. "What?"

Before I could help myself, I'd stood, pushing away from the table. "Are you serious?"

Maximus regarded me like I was about to make a run for it again. He shifted to stop me, but I held up a hand. I wasn't going to run away. Not now at least.

"You want me—*me!*—to be your savior? To stop all of you from bickering? To unite the lot of you for the rest of time?" The words sounded even stupider coming out of my mouth than theirs. What the hell were they thinking? What was I thinking? This wasn't a new home or a fresh start. They wanted someone I could never be. I wasn't a savior, a mediator, or anything like the woman they wanted. If they'd chosen me, they'd chosen wrong.

"And you thought *I* was crazy?" I laughed. I couldn't help it. This was just so ridiculous.

The four of them looked back at me with wide

eyes. It was almost comical, especially with Jett's grin wiped from his face.

"We know you're not crazy," Owen said quietly.

"Speak for your own damn self," Jett said.

Owen shot him a glare that could wither bone. "Shut up, Jett."

"Enough," Maximus growled. He turned to face me. "Yes, you are supposed to be the savior of the clans and unite us all for the rest of eternity. But you aren't expected to do it alone."

"And we don't expect you to do it right this minute," Cash added.

I looked between the two of them, mildly surprised by Maximus's attempt to soothe me without being condescending or calling me an animal. My wolf hummed her approval as I assessed the man who was supposed to be my mate. For the first time, he wasn't being a giant jerk.

"But I get why you'd doubt it," he said.

He just had to go and ruin it.

I narrowed my eyes at him and barely held back a growl. Whether the chocolate milk had been a peace offering or some attempt at bribery, I suddenly wanted to throw the delicious drink in his smug face. If I had more than a mouthful left, I might have.

I took a deep breath to calm myself, tearing away from Maximus's gaze. "So what happens now?"

"You stay here," Maximus said immediately.

I resisted rolling my eyes. I still wasn't sure if I was

okay with that, though I doubted I had much of a choice. If I was some sort of mystic shifter prophesied to save the clans, they'd never let me get far on my own. And the more time I spent under their intense gazes, the more I was warming to the idea of staying. Even as my confusing wolf continued to chant *mine, mine, mine, mine* as I looked at each of them, my heart clenched with uncertainty.

"It couldn't hurt to stay for awhile," I said.

Maximus's warm exhale hit my arm, even with more than a foot between us. The others exchanged relieved glances, and even Jett seemed to relax.

"But, I have some conditions."

Maximus froze like a deer in headlights. "Conditions?"

"Yes." I sat back down and crossed my arms. "No more cages is the first."

"Of course," Owen answered for Maximus, who shot him a glare.

"Agreed?" I prodded.

Maximus sighed. "As long as you don't go feral or try to run off again."

"Fine." I pursed my lips as I thought of what else I might want. "I want to be able to come and go from the lodge as I please."

Maximus opened his mouth to protest.

I beat him to it, my temper flaring. "I should be every bit as free as you."

"You are," Owen said.

I stared down Maximus. "I won't go too far, but I won't stay locked up. If you treat me like a prisoner, I'll act like one. Which means I'll try to escape every chance I get."

"What else?" Maximus asked.

I smiled. "I want chocolate milk every morning."

His lips twitched at the corners, but before he could smile, he pushed it back with a scowl. "Is that all?"

I looked up as I thought, taking a few more moments than necessary just to make him sweat. "That's all." I gave him a serene smile before adding, "For now."

"If that's it," Cash said, "Then I think it's time we discuss a plan to visit the other clans' territories."

"Already?" Maximus grumbled.

"It's customary," Cash said.

I looked between them, excitement bubbling inside me. In the pits, I knew I'd been missing out on a lot. When my wolf took over, I could sometimes smell the distant scent of pine trees and the salt of the sea. I'd never pictured a world where I'd be free, able to travel and see things beyond my tiny cell. And here they were discussing a trip like it was nothing.

My fingers tightened around the hem of my t-shirt, and I bit the inside of my cheek to keep from smiling too widely. It was just hitting me, but I could already almost believe it. I was finally free.

## 9
## ARIANA

After the meeting, Jett took his leave pretty quickly. The other two alphas seemed reluctant to go.

"You need all the protection you can get around here," Owen said. "You don't know if Dante will send someone after her. He must be pissed that he's losing money without her."

"He was risking her life every night," Maximus said. "He shouldn't be too torn up about it."

"I'm right here, guys," I said, rolling my eyes.

"What do you think?" Owen asked, turning his kind eyes on me.

I paused, surprised. No one had asked what I thought about any of this. I was their prized political pawn, apparently, but so far, that hadn't led to a whole lot of respect.

"Dante won't give up his claim that easily," I said. "He

owned me because I was born while my parents were his property. That makes me his property. He probably wouldn't kill me if he found me here, but he'd kill you."

"Seems like everyone wants a piece of our Ari," Cash said with a wink.

His comment spread through me like warm honey, sweetening my blood.

"*My* Ari," Maximus snapped.

My wolf growled back at him. Maximus may have thought I was his, but my wolf thought the ownership went the other way.

"She's your mate," Owen said, holding up both hands in surrender. "No one's denying that."

"I might be denying it," I grumbled. "Don't I get a say in this?"

"Of course," Owen said. "No one's going to force you do anything you aren't ready for."

"Thank you," I said, my fingers itching to reach out and take his hand.

"It's customary for the Silver Shifter to be mated to the alpha of whatever clan she's born into," Maximus said.

"Hm." I scrunched my lips to one side. "I wasn't born into a clan."

*All mine...*hummed my wolf.

*Yes, I know you think they're all yours, you greedy bitch.*

"But...you're a wolf," Maximus said, looking taken

aback. "Are you telling me your wolf doesn't think she's my mate?"

"She might," I admitted. *But she also thinks I have three others.* I kept the words to myself, though they didn't ring any less true.

Maximus smiled, and again, I noticed how gorgeous he was when he smiled. His sculpted features relaxed, and he lost that irritating habit of looking like he wanted to snap my head off.

I didn't hold back my smile in return.

Cash cleared his throat. "So, you're okay with us sticking around for a few days? To increase security, of course."

"Don't you have a job to get back to?" Maximus asked, shooting him a look.

Cash grinned. "Lucky for you, my laptop's in the car, and I can work anywhere."

"Lucky me," Maximus muttered.

"Good deal," Owen said, rising from the table. "Then it's all settled. I'll toss my bag in one of the guest rooms."

"You brought a bag?" Maximus asked.

"Yeah," Owen said, shrugging. "I was a Boy Scout. Always be prepared. And thanks for your hospitality, man. I appreciate it."

He held out a hand, and after a slight hesitation, Maximus clasped it. When Owen and Cash went out to get their things, I stood up, too. I was itching for some fresh air. Being stuck in a cage for years did that to a girl.

"I'm going for a walk," I said.

"Alone?"

I rolled my eyes. "Yes, Maximus. Alone."

"I was hoping... maybe I could join you?"

"Wait, hold up," I said. "Is the great Alpha Maximus asking my permission to do something?" I couldn't hold back my teasing smile.

"Yeah," he said, his shoulders slumping. "I guess I am."

"Okay," I said, feeling strangely shy now that he hadn't pushed to control me. I didn't know how to relate to him when we weren't fighting.

Shira appeared in the doorway holding a shoe box and a package of socks. She glanced between us like she was afraid she was interrupting something. "Here are your things, Ariana."

"Wow," I said, taking them from her. "Does everything I need just appear in this house?"

"Not so bad having an alpha for a mate now, is it?" Maximus asked smugly.

Just when I'd thought he might stop being a dick.

Shira rolled her eyes, letting me know I wasn't the only one who'd noticed, and I grinned back at her. As I pulled on the brand new socks, my toes wiggled in appreciation. I wasn't used to having new things. I threw open the lid to the shoebox and pulled on the brand new pair of running shoes in just my size.

"Are these yours?" I looked at Shira for confirmation from my seat on a bench.

"No," she said. "They're all yours."

"Where'd you get them?"

Her eyes flitted over my head to Maximus, and I twisted around. "You got me these?" I asked. "How'd you know my size?"

"Lucky guess." He shrugged.

"There are more clothes for you upstairs," Shira said. "I would have brought them down, but I thought it'd be a nice surprise for later." She winked, and my cheeks heated.

I turned back to Maximus, a lump in my throat. I couldn't remember the last time anyone bought me anything. "Thank you."

"Of course. You need your own things." He gave me a tight-lipped smile and then turned to Shira. "Will you get the other alphas set up in the guest rooms? It seems we'll be having company for a few days."

"Sure thing," Shira said. "Both of them?" She could barely contain her smile, which did not go unnoticed by my wolf. I wrestled to keep her from bursting out of my human form and leaping onto Shira.

Shira must have noticed the expression on my face, because she dropped her voice and squeezed my arm. "Obviously they can't have a wolf for a mate, but that doesn't mean they're not fun to look at. Am I right?"

She gave me a wink, and I forced a smile, even as

my wolf growled her usual *mine, mine, mine,* chant. I joined Maximus at the door, and just as we stepped outside, the other two arrived with their things.

"We're going out for a while," Maximus said to them. "Shira will show you to your rooms."

"If you want to wait a minute, we'll join you," Cash said.

I opened my mouth to invite them both to come, but Maximus spoke before I could.

"Maybe next time." His hand closed around my arm in a possessive but gentle hold. "You don't want to keep the lady waiting, do you?"

He led me from the porch, frowning when he noticed me glancing over my shoulder at the two men we were leaving. "Let me show you around the property," he said, his hand sliding down my arm. He surprised me by linking his hand with mine. "With all the excitement, I've hardly had a moment alone with you."

I considered this. Everything had happened so fast, I hadn't even realized it. Maximus was supposed to be my mate, and yet we hadn't spent a second without someone else hovering. I twisted my lip between my teeth as I thought about his fingers linked with mine and what it meant.

"What about Shira?" I asked. "She's not...I mean, was she your mate before I got here?"

"No," he said with a frown. "Wolves only have one mate. It's customary for a second to live with the alpha if they're both unmated, but we aren't involved in that way."

*Mine, all mine*, my wolf said with approval.

"Good," I said, my fingers tightening around his. When we stepped into the woods, the heat of the sun on my shoulders disappeared as the leaves overhead shaded the path. The trail I'd followed before my encounter with Cash was narrow but well worn, dappled with sunlight in the daytime.

"Is it?" Maximus asked, his eyes searching mine. "Good that I'm single, I mean. It seems like we got off on the wrong foot somewhere. I get the feeling you don't like me very much."

I narrowed my eyes. "You locked me in a cage."

His jaw tightened. "And I apologized."

"Did you?"

He sighed and raked a hand through his hair. "If I didn't, I'm sorry. This is all new to me, too. I had to make a split second decision that would be best for the whole pack. Obviously it wasn't the best thing for me."

Best thing for him?

I scoffed. "You weren't the one locked in the basement."

"I'm the one dealing with the consequences," he countered.

We came out at the spot where I'd climbed the cliffs and fallen. The afternoon sun cast a warm glow over the exposed bluffs.

"I'm only human," Maximus said, tugging my hand so I had to stop and face him. "Well, not *only* human. But I'm equally fallible. Do you think you can forgive me?"

My heart softened at the glimpse of vulnerability in him that I hadn't seen before. "I think I can do that," I said, my voice a little breathless.

"I want you to have your freedom," Maximus said, his voice dropping. He stepped closer and reached for me, his fingers sliding across my cheek and slowly winding a strand of silver hair behind my ear. "I don't mean to be impatient. But I've been waiting my whole life for my mate."

Something between us shifted in that moment. I knew that my wolf wanted Maximus, and I knew he wanted me for his mate. Now that I knew what this meant, warmth spread through me, and my legs threatened to give way. It was a lot of pressure.

"Just don't rush me into this, okay, Maximus?"

He swallowed before nodding. "You're right," he said. "I'm not thinking of what life was like for you. There's no rush. I hope you know that."

"Good," I said with a little gulp. I'd never experienced anything close to intimacy, and the thought of it was daunting, though I couldn't deny that both my wolf and my human body were excited by the prospect. It was my human mind that balked.

"But you're still my mate," he said, sliding his hand

to the back of my neck. The scent of pine trees and crisp air surrounded me—the smell of Maximus.

"You just don't know when to stop, do you?" I whispered, letting him pull me even closer. I could see the flecks of green and gold and chestnut in his eyes, the length of his thick black lashes, the shadow of stubble on his strong jaw.

"Stop what?" he asked, his breath tickling my lips.

"Stop being an alpha."

"No," he said, and then his lips were on mine.

I drew a shaky breath as his mouth moved against mine, soft at first, then more insistent. My lips responded, following his lead instinctually. My hands fisted in his T-shirt, my body collapsing into his. His hands fell to my waist, drawing me gently but firmly against him. After a minute, his tongue touched my lip and I gasped, parting my lips. His tongue pressed into my mouth, sliding slowly and rhythmically against mine. Heat coiled in my belly, spreading downwards, filling my core with a need I'd never known.

Suddenly, my wolf sprang to life inside me, growling for more. Without thinking, my teeth sank into his tongue.

"Fuck," Maximus said, drawing away and wiping the back of his hand across his lips. Then a smile began to spread across his face and his eyebrow quirked up. "Did you just try to claim me?"

My cheeks heated. "Isn't that what you want?"

His smile dropped away, and his eyes fixed on my

lips with such longing it made me shiver in the best way. "Very much," he said, his voice husky.

That slightest taste of his blood lingered on my tongue, but it wasn't enough. My wolf was practically ripping through my skin for more, and I wasn't sure I could stop her.

"You'll be part of the pack," he said. "Permanently this time. But I can protect you this way. Of course it's what I want, Ariana."

"Me too," I breathed, standing on my tiptoes and stretching up to him again.

He took a step forward, pushing me back against a tree that grew beside the path. This time, his kiss was deeper, more commanding. He slid a hand behind my head, cushioning it from the rough bark as his tongue swept across mine. My teeth clamped down on his tongue, and he moaned softly into my mouth. A second later, he sucked my lip between his teeth, and I drew a sharp breath, pleasure rippling through me.

My wolf shuddered her approval.

Maximus's teeth bit down gently on my lower lip, pressing harder until the skin broke. I gasped, my body arching against his, electrified. As my blood mixed with his on my tongue, dizzying pleasure swept through my body and my knees gave way. Maximus's body caught mine, his hips pinning mine against the tree. Heat throbbed between my trembling thighs as the flavor of our blood mingled on my tongue, creating something new and right. The taste of us, together.

"My god, Ari," he whispered, breaking the kiss. His hand fisted in my hair, his forehead pressed to mine. "If you want me to be able to stop, you'd better let me do it now."

My hand flattened on his chest. I could feel his heart hammering under my palm, pounding in rhythm with my own. "Then we should stop," I said, though my wolf howled in protest inside me.

Maximus nodded, stepping back to separate his body from mine.

"It's just, I've never even been kissed," I whispered breathlessly.

"You don't have to explain."

"Is it always like that?"

He closed his eyes and exhaled. "Never."

## 10

## ARIANA

A week later, we headed away from the wolf mountain. My heart pounded with excitement as I gazed out the window at the overcast sky and trees swaying in the wind. I was excited to see the other clans, but I'd gotten more comfortable with the wolves, too. They'd all welcomed me, and as Maximus's mate, they treated me as someone important. That took some getting used to, but I was starting to settle in. Shira had continued working with me on putting up my defenses so the wolves weren't always in my mind. I could still hear Maximus because he was the alpha but only when he wanted me to.

Cash's silver Lincoln led the way down the winding road, followed by Maximus's Jeep and Owen's truck.

"You're going to love the dragons," Cash said,

shooting me a grin. "I can't wait for you to meet everyone."

Much to Maximus's annoyance, I'd chosen to ride with Cash. I wanted to get the first glimpse of the place the dragon clan called home.

"Are they like the wolves?" I asked.

"Not really," Cash said. "But I don't want to spoil it for you. Just wait and see."

"Do you live on a mountain like that, though? Up in the woods where humans won't see you?"

"Not exactly," he said, smirking as his hands tapped the steering wheel.

I sighed and turned to the window, frustrated with people keeping me in the dark. Now that I was in the same enclosed space as Cash, his scent overwhelmed me—bonfires, and cinnamon. And annoyingly distracting, considering Max was my mate.

I ran my fingers along the edge of the supple leather seat, breathing through my mouth as I tried to push out the delicious smell and focus on the car. Even on the dirt road, the Lincoln had provided a smooth ride. Now that we were on the highway, I could barely tell I was moving.

"It must be even harder for you to hide, since you fly," I said. "The others aren't as conspicuous."

"Must be boring to be earthbound," he said. "But don't worry. I'll give you a lift any time, sweetheart."

I started to protest the use of that word, but my wolf preened at being given a nickname. "I might take you up on that," I said. "It must be an even better view than climbing the cliffs."

"You have no idea," he said. "Just don't tell Maximus you're riding me. He might not like that."

"It's not his place to tell me who I can or cannot ride." I crossed my arms.

Cash grinned at the road ahead. "Good to know."

We turned into the city, where metal behemoths loomed in the distance. My heartbeat quickened. I'd never seen much of the city. I'd forgotten how the skyscrapers brushed the clouds. Maximus's presence brushed across my mind, checking that I was okay. Warmth swelled inside me. We'd butted heads a few times over the past week, but things had smoothed out considerably since I joined the pack.

As we turned onto a narrow street, a black SUV surged out of an alley straight in front of us. Cash swore and slammed on the brakes. The heels of my palms slammed into the dashboard, then my body lurched back against the seat. Behind us, Maximus's tires squealed as he came to a stop just inches from our bumper. Another SUV barreled out of the alley on the other side, blocking off that lane, too. The whole road was blocked, and more SUVS were crawling out of alleyways and joining the two blocking the road in front and behind us. Blocking us in.

Adrenaline burst through me as the door to one of the vehicles opened, and a tall, impossibly pale man with jet black hair stepped out.

"Shit," I whispered, leaning forward and gripping the dash as more men spilled from the cars ahead. "Vampires."

"Stay here!" Cash barked.

My wolf bristled at being told what to do, but the rest of me stared at the familiar vampire in horror. Cold fear slithered through my belly and down my spine. I knew that vampire. I knew his violent hands just as well as I knew the smirk on his face. He was one of the pit guards. One of Dante's men.

My fists clenched around the hem of my shirt. All I could do was watch as Cash leapt out of the car and slammed the door shut. Smoke blew from his nostrils as he stepped in front of the nose of the car.

I felt Maximus's presence in my head, commanding me to stay, like some kind of dog. If I weren't so terrified, I might have argued. But as the red eyes of the pit guard met mine, the whole world drained away. The last week didn't exist. I'd never met the four handsome alphas or heard of the New York Clans.

I was back in the pits, the dirt coarse beneath my paws, cold air licking my fur, and fear gripping my spine as a metal baton clanged against the bars of the cage across from mine.

*Clang. Clang. Clang.*

The baton hit bar after bar, and I winced at each sound. I scurried back in my small cage, pinning myself to the opposite side. A sharp whistle cut through the air, and crimson eyes peered into the dark recesses of my prison.

*"Hello, little doggie."* His voice sent a shiver through my entire body.

And then I was back, sitting inside Cash's car, shaking. Vampires surrounded the alpha dragon. Where were Maximus and Owen?

Tearing myself from the vampire's gaze, I turned in my seat. Out the rear window I could see more bloodsuckers surrounding Maximus's SUV. Maximus and Owen were already out of the car, surrounded by vampires. My wolf snarled, ready to join them.

*No one harms my mates.*

Before I could think about what I was doing, I thrust the car door open and leapt out.

Cash gave me with an irritated glare as I strode to his side, my fists clenched. I forced myself to take deep breaths and face down one of the many vampires to terrorize me for the last few years.

"There she is," the vampire purred. His lips pulled back to reveal his fangs. "Dante sends his regards, little doggie."

Anger burned through me, and my wolf fought against my skin. I just barely held her in check. "Tell him to shove his regards up his ass," I growled.

The man's eyebrows shot up in surprise. I'd never talked back before, but then again, I'd been a wolf for the last couple years. "My, my." He chuckled darkly. "Doggie has more than just bite." His gaze trailed me up and down before settling back on my face. "Come, girl. Time to go home to your master."

"She isn't going anywhere." Cash stepped in front of me, shielding me with his body.

The vampire's eyes flashed as he sniffed the air. "A dragon?"

"Damn right," Cash growled.

"It seems you've made some new friends."

My nostrils flared and my fists balled. Before I could respond, the vampire raised his hand and motioned forward with two fingers. "Take her."

My heart leapt as a dozen vampires surged toward us. Cash roared as wings flew from his back, shredding his dress shirt. His wings slammed into the first few vampires to reach us and sent them flying back toward the SUVs.

"Get back in the car!" Cash commanded.

Both me and my wolf rolled our eyes in amusement.

*Not fucking happening.*

Instinct took over, and when the first vampire slipped past Cash, I slammed my fist into his cheek. I might have been a wolf for the last two years, but when my father had still been alive he'd taught me a thing or two about hand-to-hand combat.

The vampire stilled. Instead of being thrown back like my father had been in our practice matches, he barely moved. Only his face moved to the side with the impact. The rest of him remained like a statue.

Shit.

"Ariana!" Cash barked.

I leapt back as the vampire rounded on me again. This wasn't good. I had to transform. My wolf was a far better fighter than human Ariana.

"Come here, little girl," another vampire hissed through his teeth as he grabbed my arm and yanked me away from Cash and his gigantic wings.

The dragon alpha sent blazing trails of red, orange and yellow through the air as he launched fireballs at the vampires. But it wasn't enough. Shifters might be fast, but vampires were faster, and they far outnumbered us.

I yanked my arm from the vampire's grasp and stomped on his foot before slamming my elbow into his nose. Pain shot up my arm. It was like hitting concrete.

The vampire grabbed me again, this time restraining me with both hands on my biceps. My wolf howled for release, but just as I went to unleash her, giving her control in this awful situation, pain shot through my neck.

I cried out in shock.

A draining feeling washed through my veins, like my very life was being sucked from inside me, and I lost the grip on my transformation.

I'd never been fed on by a vampire, and I didn't like it one bit. I thrashed in the vampire's grasp until he pulled back breathlessly.

"You're far tastier than I imagined, pretty puppy."

Disgust turned my stomach, and again I tried to pull away, but his grip was like iron. Another vampire joined him, and then another.

Heat coursed through me as their bites tore through my flesh. The world spun, and stars danced at the edge of my vision. My body started to go numb, the pain falling away as my legs gave out.

Distantly I heard someone calling my name, and in one last attempt, I sent out a desperate mental plea for Maximus to get this bloodsucking leach away from me.

## 11

## MAXIMUS

Pain and terror shot through the pack bond like a wave of ice water. I gasped and threw the vampire atop me away, scrambling to my feet to look for who dared to harm my mate.

My heart raced as I saw all the blood and ash at my feet. I'd killed a few vampires that stood in my path already, but there had to be nearly a dozen on this end alone. The second I'd leapt from my car, I'd tried to get to Ariana, but the vampires had crowded in, separating me from my mate.

I'd been foolish to relent when she'd insisted on riding with Cash. She should have been by my side when this happened. At least then I could protect her. From here, I was all but useless.

A snarl ripped from between my teeth. Blood sprayed the ground as Owen ripped off the head of another bloodsucker with his bear teeth. He'd transformed almost before he was out of his truck. The man was a good fighter, and I was glad to have him by my side, but it didn't stop me from wishing it was Ariana instead.

"Give up now, wolfie," a female vampire purred. I was sure the sound was supposed to be sexy, but it only grated against my ears and made me want to tear her head off.

"Unlikely, nightwalker." I leapt over the pile of ash at my feet and reached for her shoulder, intent on throwing her across the street.

She dodged to the side, a blur of movement, and backhanded me. Pain shot through me as I spun through the air and landed hard on the hood of my Jeep. Breath exploded from my lungs, and I barely rolled off before the vampire landed in my place, her hand leaving an outline of her knuckles on my new blue paint job.

*Son of a bitch.*

I growled as I grabbed her ankle and yanked her foot out from under her and pulled her off my car and onto the pavement. She screeched and her booted foot lashed out to stab me with her heel. I grabbed her other ankle and threw her over my head and across the street. Her scream echoed between buildings as she flew, and I heard a loud crash as she sailed through the glass window of an ice cream joint.

Fuck. Ariana's pained cry was no longer in my head.

"You good?" I shouted at Owen, who'd just charged a group of vampires.

He barely glanced back, giving a swift nod before his hulking grizzly form stood on his hind legs and swiped enormous claws at the vampires before him.

I turned and raced between cars, sliding over the dented hood of my Jeep before taking off to find Ariana. Her voice was gone from my head, but her presence was still there. She wasn't dead, though every fiber of my wolf howled for me to kill every last being that dared lay a hand on her.

Cash roared up ahead, spraying fire at the surrounding pack of vampires. I stopped by the head of his Lincoln and scanned the flaming ash for signs of Ariana.

*There!* A flash of silver caught my eye between a huddle of vampires. Before I could stop my wolf, I was transforming. My body cracked and reshaped, but past the momentary pain, all I saw was red.

Ariana's limp body was cradled between three feasting bloodsuckers. Long trails of blood streamed from her exposed neck, dripping over her collarbones before disappearing into her shirt.

I snarled in rage as I leapt across the pavement and barrelled into the first vampire. Surprise registered in his glazed eyes, and then I had his throat between my teeth. I yanked my head up with one swift jerk. The disgusting taste of vampires—the taste of ash—filled my mouth, and I spit it out as his severed head hit the street a few feet away.

I spun to face the others. They'd dropped my mate on the ground and turned to face me. I lunged at the closest vampire.

He caught me mid-air and threw me to the side. Pain shot down my spine as my back hit a group of metal mailboxes. I forced back the pain and leapt aside before either of them reached me. Neither blurred with movement as they usually did. The same glazed look was in their cold eyes. One vampire shot forward, followed slowly by the other. They got caught in each other's way, giving me time to snap the ankles of the first with my powerful jaws. He tumbled to the ground, and the second fell on top of him with a grunt.

I leapt onto his back and sank my teeth into his shoulder. He screeched as I dug in harder, my claws ripping through his shirt and then his skin. The sound continued to echo off the surrounding buildings until I finally severed his spinal cord. His body fell limp on top of his friend.

I pulled back to throw the body away, but the vampire was faster, throwing the body of his comrades at me before racing down the closest alley.

My wolf was torn between chasing the vampires and going to Ari, but my human knew Ari was my end and my beginning. I ran to her, my breath strangled in my throat. She lay in a heap in the middle of the street, her silver hair spilling over her face and blood covering the front of her shirt. A whimper escaped me, and I scrambled to reach her side as fast as I could.

I shifted back to my human form and fell to my knees at Ariana's side. My hands froze inches from touching her. I didn't want to harm her further, but I had to know she was okay.

Carefully, I pushed her hair back, away from her neck. Her shirt was ripped and stretched from where the vampires had grabbed her, but other than the bites on her neck and shoulders, she didn't have any other injuries.

I took her in my arms, cradling her in my lap.

"Ariana," I whispered, brushing strands of hair from her face. My heart thundered in my chest. I'd just found her, and I couldn't lose her, not like this. "Ari."

After a long moment, her eyelids fluttered open, and the swirling silver depths of her eyes were revealed. I heaved a sigh of relief and clutched her to me, pressing my heart to hers.

"Damn it, Ariana," I growled. "Don't ever do that again."

Soft fingers brushed my shoulder, and I froze before pulling back to look at her.

"Do what?" Her voice was tiny, quiet, like she could barely speak.

I tightened my grip. "Ariana?"

Cash dropped to his knees on her other side. "Ari, are you all right?"

"Hey!" Owen called. "They're backing off."

He trotted over to join us, jeans slung around his hips, blond hair a dishevelled mess. He set a folded pair of pants beside me, and I glanced down at them in surprise.

"The vampires have retreated," Cash confirmed. "We need to get the Silver Shifter out of here."

I nodded my agreement. I could barely take my eyes off her as her eyelids continued to flutter. It was clear she fought to stay conscious. "Rest," I told her, pressing a gentle kiss to her forehead.

Ariana closed her eyes and leaned her head against my arm, seeming content that she was safe.

"What the hell was that?" Owen asked. He shifted from foot to foot, glancing at every shadow like another vampire might leap from it.

"I don't know," Cash said. His jaw hardened as he stood, inspecting the street for further danger.

"Come on, we should go," Owen said.

I stood, my heart clenching painfully in my chest. This had been a close call. Something was wrong. Dante might be wealthy and well connected, but how had he known we'd come this way in the first place?

Was it just luck? Or something more?

I ground my teeth as the same thoughts circled my head again and again. If someone had betrayed us, I wouldn't rest until they were found and dealt with.

## 12

## ARIANA

I woke up in a moving car. Even in human form, I could smell blood. "Maximus?" I mumbled. "Cash? Owen?"

"You doing roll call?" a deep voice rumbled above me.

"Owen," I whispered, closing my hand over his knee. My head rested on his thigh as I lay across the seat of his truck.

"Everyone's alive," he said, dropping one hand from the steering wheel to my shoulder. "You and Maximus got the worst of it. I'm taking you back to his place because it's closest."

I drifted off again, comforted by his presence. He was like a mountain, that man. In his hands, I felt completely safe in a way I didn't feel anywhere else. It was a safety I hadn't felt since curling up in my mother's arms as a child, before I even knew what it meant to be in a warlock's debt. There was a conviction to that comfort, an unwavering belief that nothing bad could happen as long as I was loved.

Which was strange, because of course Owen didn't love me. We'd spent a little time together over the past week, but I didn't know him as well as Maximus and Cash. Owen seemed content to stand back and watch Cash flirt with me and Maximus try to boss me around. He was always kind and respectful, but we hadn't spent any time alone together.

I woke when he lifted me out of his truck. Night had fallen, and a cool breeze blew a strand of my silver hair across my face as Owen carried me towards the lodge, cradling me in his arms like a baby. I wound my arms around his neck, laying my head on his warm, solid chest.

All around, the pack was rushing to help Maximus out of the car, pelting him with questions and concerns about his well being.

"Let's get you to bed," Owen said, his voice rumbling through his body and mine. Even though I was barely conscious, my wolf and my human were in agreement—it felt right to be in Owen's arms, like coming home at last.

"Where's Cash?" I managed as Owen carried me up the stairs.

"He went home," Owen said. "He had a few injuries, but he's going to be fine. He just needed a doctor familiar with dragon anatomy."

"Oh," I said, relieved that he was getting the best care he could. "What about you?"

"I shifted early," Owen said, opening the door to the bedroom where I'd been staying. "I didn't get hurt much. You just worry about getting yourself better, all right?"

Dante's face flashed in my mind. I swallowed hard, my limbs trembling. I didn't know how I could ever feel safe with him out there. Now that he knew where I was, who I was with, he'd be coming for me. Hunting me.

When Owen laid me on the bed, I kept my arms around his neck, tugging him close. He was so strong he'd escaped the vampires with barely more than a scratch.

"Stay with me?" I whispered.

"Ariana..."

I closed my eyes. "Please? Just hold me until I fall asleep."

He hesitated, then stood and went to the door. My chest squeezed, and I curled up into a ball, holding my hands under my chin, trying to hold in the hurt. I'd learned long ago not to ask for anything. It only let someone else see your vulnerability, your need.

Owen paused for a second in the doorway, then shut off the light and pushed the door closed.

"Maximus won't like this," he muttered as he approached the bed. I felt his weight sinking onto the mattress, and then he swung his legs up and lay down beside me.

"It's not Maximus's choice," I said, fitting my body into the angles of his. I sighed, amazed by how well we fit, how right it felt. "It's my choice. You're my choice."

"That's the blood loss talking," he said, his voice so low it was a rumble beneath the surface, more felt than heard. His massive arm snaked around me, pulling my body to his. Lying with him like this, I felt how fragile I had become while in the pits. He could have broken me with his bare hands. And yet, I'd never felt so safe in my life. I knew instinctively that he would use that strength to protect me, never turning it against me.

I snuggled closer into his arms, pressing back into his lap and sliding my fingers through his, holding his arm around me.

"Tell me you don't feel it," I mumbled, my eyes falling closed. "Tell me this doesn't feel right."

"It feels right," he admitted, his voice barely audible. "But..."

"Shhhh," I said, smiling in the darkness, letting the exhaustion melt my body into the bed, into him. "I'm trying to sleep."

Owen's chuckle rumbled through my entire body, and his embrace tightened. I disappeared into the black behind my eyelids before I could hear his response.

I woke to find myself still cocooned against Owen's body. The scent of sandalwood clung to my nose and heated my insides. My body was a little sore, and my clothes stuck to me in all the wrong place, but I'd slept the whole night protected and safe in his arms. Before now, the only person who had made me feel safe was Maximus, and that was different...or was it? Turning it over in my mind, I tried to find a way in which my mate felt better, safer, or more right than this. But it felt exactly the same.

The thought startled me. I shouldn't even be capable of feeling this way about someone after claiming a mate. And yet, it felt just as right, just as perfect, just as simple.

*Mine...*

My wolf growled in pleasure at the sensations of Owen's body pressed so tightly against mine. He was breathing deeply, his arms wrapped snugly around me. His body was relaxed in sleep, but something much less relaxed was pressing firmly against my ass. I drew a slow breath as I realized what it was. I'd never been in this kind of situation before. I'd spent my teenage years in a freaking cage with a dirt floor. My curiosity burned through me, and I struggled around under his arm to face him. Tentatively, I ran my fingertip down his chest.

Owen's eyes fluttered open, and my heartbeat

increased. I gulped, but he didn't stop my finger from moving lower, over his abs, until it reached the top of his jeans. Slowly, I moved lower, tracing the outline of his erection with my fingernail.

By the time I'd finished, more than curiosity was burning through me. My breath was coming faster, shallower, and so was his. Our eyes locked, and I inhaled sharply when I read the desire in his eyes.

"Ariana," he breathed. "We can't. You're..." He broke off, swallowing hard.

"I'm what?" I whispered.

"You're injured," he said, taking my hand and lacing my fingers through his. His big hands were work-worn and calloused, his skin hot against mine. "And you're Maximus's mate. Do you have any idea how pissed he'd be if he knew this was going on?"

"And what about you?" I asked. "What do you want?"

"That doesn't matter."

"Then what about your bear? What does he want?"

"My bear...is a little confused right now," Owen said.

"How so?" I asked, my heart suddenly hammering again. I wanted to hear him say it, to know that my inner animal wasn't the only one confused in this way.

"He thinks you're our mate," Owen admitted.

The relief was immediate and stronger than I'd expected. I didn't realize how conflicted I'd been until

I heard my own suspicions confirmed. I closed my eyes, my head swimming with dizziness. Owen propped himself up on his elbow. "Ariana? Are you okay? I didn't mean to upset you. I shouldn't have said anything."

"Not...upset," I said. "But maybe I should eat something."

"On it," Owen said, rolling up from the bed to his feet. A minute after he padded from the room, Shira appeared at my bedside.

"Maximus wants you to quit blocking him so completely from your thoughts," she said with a small smile.

"Tell Maximus to stay in his own head," I said. "And that I'm fine."

"Do you need anything?"

"Owen's getting me food."

"Hmm," she said. "Interesting."

"I know I'm Maximus's mate," I said. "But there's something else going on. I don't know yet. Just tell him he doesn't have to worry."

She studied me a minute. "Okay," she said at last. "I sense that you're doing what's best for the pack. I don't know how that can be, but you must know what you're doing."

When she left, I closed my eyes and rested a moment. I appreciated her trust, but I didn't know if I deserved it. I had no idea what I was doing.

After I ate, I spent most of the day sleeping and

recovering from the attack. Owen stayed by my side all day, and Maximus came in to visit as well. By evening, I felt stronger when I woke.

"Want me to bring you up some dinner?" Owen asked. He was sitting in the chair where I'd been piling my clothes all week.

"Maybe," I said, pushing myself up to sit. When I yawned and stretched, I felt the tightness of my shirt. Looking down, I realized I was still covered in blood from the night before. I shuddered and peeled off the shirt without thinking. Owen averted his eyes, his cheeks going a little red. Around the others, I would have felt like they were staring, and I would have immediately felt self-conscious. But when Owen sat staring at the floor, I realized I wanted him to look at me.

My wolf was growling things that didn't make sense, and my body was just as bad. My cold skin quivered at the thought of Owen's rough, hot fingers on it.

"I should get cleaned up," I said, bewildered by my own thoughts and desires. I clambered from the bed, and Owen rushed to my side. He scooped me into his arms and carried me to the bathroom. A large, clawfoot tub sat in the middle of the floor, and Owen drew back the curtain and turned on the water.

"Can you sit up in the bath?" he asked.

"I think so," I said, though my legs felt like noodles when I stood. I looked into the rushing water, and suddenly I was lying on the pavement again, blood trickling down my neck, wetting my shirt. I turned away from the water and sank onto the edge of the tub. Swallowing hard, I avoided Owen's eyes as I spoke. "Will you stay?"

"Take as much time as you need, Ariana."

I nodded, gripping the button of my jeans. "Will you?"

"Of course," he said, crouching beside me. His big hand rested gently on my lower back, his eyes searching my face. "I'm going to take care of you."

I knew, somehow, that his words extended beyond this moment. That he was promising something that had nothing to do with my weakness or injuries. Sometime during the day, he must have began to listen to his bear as seriously as I was listening to my wolf.

I nodded mutely, my throat suddenly tight. His hand felt hot against my bare skin, and I was suddenly aware of how close we were, that I could feel the heat of him climbing my arms, my ribs, warming my chest. Owen knelt and undid my jeans, slowly working them down over my hips and thighs. His lips were set in a determined, businesslike expression.

When I looked down, I saw that my underwear were caught in my jeans, sliding down with them.

My breath caught, and I rested my hands on his shoulders for balance while he tugged my jeans over my feet. He lifted his gaze, his eyes catching between my thighs. He swallowed and raised his eyes to mine.

My fingers curled into the shoulders of his shirt, tugging him closer. His large, calloused hands closed around the back of my calves, sliding up to the soft skin behind my knees. Heat raced up my thighs, curling into a knot of anticipation at my core. I closed my eyes, drawing a shaky breath.

"Let's get you in the tub," Owen said, his voice low but gruff. He stood quickly, lifting me and easing my body gently into the warm water.

I reached behind my back and undid my bra, sliding it over my arms and dropping it beside the tub. Owen grabbed a bottle of bubble bath and dumped half of it under the tap. A mountain of bubbles began to billow up.

"Are you trying to hide me under those?" I asked, not sure if I wanted to be hidden. Everything was happening so fast. I'd just claimed Maximus a week ago, and now, my wolf was howling for me to claim another mate. But she didn't want to give up Maximus. No, she wasn't replacing him. She was...supplementing him.

"The bubbles are for my sake, not because..." Owen's voice dropped even more. "Not because I don't want to see you. You're beautiful, Ariana."

"But...?" I said, remembering the night before, when I hadn't let him protest.

"But I'm a man, and you're a beautiful woman who my bear thinks is his mate," Owen said. "It's not easy being this close and not being able to touch you."

I met his eyes, my insides trembling at the rough edge of longing in his voice.

"So touch me," I whispered.

Owen knelt beside the tub, sliding a hand behind my head to cushion it from the hard porcelain surface. His free hand moved a washcloth gently over my cheek, letting warm water run down my face and neck. He worked his way down my neck, the warm cloth caressing my shoulder. My body melted under his hands, and I sank back into his cradling hold. Slowly, he worked his way over my collarbones and down my chest. After a slight hesitation, he ran the cloth around the bottom of my breast.

My nipples hardened, and tension coiled inside me even as my body relaxed further into the warm embrace of the soapy water. I sighed and shifted, the water lapping gently around me.

"Ariana," Owen said slowly, his hands stilling. "You're Maximus's mate."

I opened my eyes to find him frowning in confusion. I knew in that moment that my wolf was right. If he'd been the one pushing for this, I would have pushed back. But he was trying to do the right thing for me, and even for Maximus, at the expense of himself. His selflessness, the fact that he'd be willing to give up his own happiness to make sure that we were happy, made me realize what my wolf alone hadn't convinced me. He would do anything for me. He felt the same about me as Maximus did.

"And yours," I said, laying a gentle hand on his forearm. "I'm your mate too, Owen."

His brows furrowed deeper. "How can that be?"

"I don't know," I said. "But I am."

After a long, long minute, he nodded, and his face relaxing into a hesitant smile. "I guess that's one way to unite the clans."

I leaned up, circling a wet arm around his neck and pulling him down to me. His mouth met mine, his tongue skillfully claiming mine without hesitation. I pulled harder, wanting him closer. He slid over the edge of the tub, the water sloshing around us as he pulled me on top of him, his lips never leaving mine. His hands glided over my back, stopping at my hips.

I wound my legs into his, my arms around his neck. My tongue danced with his, my body riding the rise and fall of his chest as he breathed. The water swayed around us under the mountain of bubbles. After a few minutes, Owen's hands moved lower, kneading the soft flesh of my bottom, crushing my hips to his. The tension in my core coiled tighter and tighter until I was squirming against him, the need in me almost painful.

Growling into his mouth, I arched against him, trying to find the relief I needed. He echoed the sound back, a sound of frustration in his throat that vibrated through his chest and buzzed along my skin. I bit down on his lip the way Maximus had done to me, and Owen's growl rose in intensity. The vibration through my body made my nipples harden against his chest, pushing me closer to the edge. I'd never felt this way before, didn't have the words to tell him what I needed. I rocked my hips against his, the water coursing around our bodies as I moved faster.

After tugging at his shirt, I pulled it away from his skin and ran my hands up under it, over the ridges of muscle on his abdomen. My nails scraped his wet, slippery skin, searching further until I found his nipples. Owen sucked in a breath, his hand sliding down my thigh and hitching my leg up. As he raked his fingers up the back of my thigh, I arched my back, giving him better access. His fingers hesitated, then began to explore my folds. I gasped as he went deeper, dipping a finger into me.

I bit down harder on his lip, tasting blood now. Sucking on his bleeding lip, I pushed back against his hand, arching my back and spreading my knees wider. With a groan, he sank his fingers all the way into me, biting down on my lip at the same time. I cried out, something pulling tight inside me until I thought I'd burst open like a ripe fruit. Owen sucked at the blood on my tongue, sliding his fingers out and then driving them deep into me again and again.

I arched my back, burying my cries of pleasure in his mouth as my pussy clenched around his fingers. He pushed deep and held, pulsing his fingers against my walls. The tension that had been building suddenly reached an unbearable level, and then, all at once, it broke. Stars bloomed behind my eyelids as waves of pleasure uncoiled through my entire body, my tightness throbbing around his fluttering fingers. Blood spread across my tongue, and I tasted him, and me, and us.

Inside me, my wolf shuddered with approval. She had claimed her second mate.

## 13

## ARIANA

Warm light caressed my cheeks the next morning, pulling me from sleep. I blinked into the golden rays, squinting at the sheer curtains. I yawned and stretched, my muscles tensing and relaxing in turn.

Owen grumbled something beside me, his face buried in the pillow, and his arm tightly wound around my waist. I couldn't help but smile. Though he might be a large bear shifter, he could still somehow be adorable while asleep.

I lay my head down and brushed dirty blond hair back over his ear. After our encounter in the bathtub, Owen hadn't wanted to go further, and for that I was thankful. Though my first and only orgasm had been explosive, I wasn't sure I was ready to take the next step, even if my wolf howled for more.

My cheeks heated and I clenched my thighs at the

memory. It felt strange to have someone be so sweet after all my years as a captive. I didn't think it was possible until I met my mates.

*Mine*, my wolf agreed.

I didn't think my wolf could get any happier. She'd already claimed two mates, and she'd purred like a cat ever since.

Owen shifted, peeking up at me, his face still half hidden by the pillow. He inspected my face so long that I had to drop his gaze.

"Good morning," he said, his voice a deep rumble even while muffled in the pillowcase.

I shivered involuntarily and shook my hair back. "Morning."

Owen raised his head to plant a kiss on my forehead before swiping his long hair back. "Did you sleep well?"

I nodded.

"Good. Are you hungry?"

My stomach growled in response. "Apparently."

He chuckled softly, and before I could pull him back down into the sheets for a little longer, he'd sprung up from bed and tugged his jeans on. "Let's get you some breakfast."

I looked from his face to the door. It had been a few days since the incident in the city, and I finally felt like myself. Though I wanted to see the others, I was afraid of what they might say. I'd barely seen Maximus, and I felt him at the edge of my thoughts constantly, poking and prodding for a way in. Every time I felt him I slammed my mental barriers down. I wasn't ready to have him in my head, seeing my thoughts, seeing Owen. I knew once I dropped my walls, both alphas would be there. How was I supposed to explain that to Maximus?

Owen pulled on his shirt while I slipped out of bed.

I'd slept in a large t-shirt and panties. I changed quickly, pulling on a pair of jeans and a long sleeve maroon shirt with a v-neck. Once we were both dressed, I hesitated by the door.

Owen grinned, flashing his perfect teeth, then opened the door. "Come on."

I sighed and took the lead like I had with our first kiss. I steeled myself as I descended the stairs, the hum of voices clear from the kitchen. I could smell Maximus and Shira, along with eggs and bacon. My stomach growled in response, and my feet carried me through the dining room doors.

Maximus looked over his shoulder, his eyes meeting mine. He stood in front of the stove, a spatula in one hand and the handle of the frying pan in the other. His smile dropped, and something unreadable flashed through his eyes. He turned away just as Shira bounced up from her seat at the island bar.

"Good morning," she said with a wide smile. "Are you feeling better?"

"Much."

"Come on, have a seat." She ushered me over to the dining room table, pulling out my seat for me.

I smiled at her and nodded my thanks as she sat down beside me. There was already a glass of chocolate milk sitting on the table, and I grabbed it hungrily.

"Breakfast smells great," Owen said as he took a seat on the other side of the table. "Anything I can do to help?"

"No," Maximus grunted. He didn't even look over his shoulder, but continued to flip eggs like he was spearing a vampire.

I sucked down my chocolate milk, wondering how they knew I'd come down today. It didn't seem like Maximus was in the best of moods, though that wasn't exactly surprising.

"Is he okay?" I whispered to Shira. He could probably hear me with his enhanced wolf hearing and all, but still I pitched my voice low.

Shira glanced between him and I. "I think you keeping him out of your head is making him anxious."

I nodded and leaned back, setting my glass back on the table. I didn't want to explain why I wasn't letting him back in. It couldn't end well for anyone, but especially not for Owen. I didn't want to cause any fights, especially on pack land where dozens of wolves might jump in to aid their leader.

Maximus finished up breakfast and set a plate in

front of each of us, though he visibly tensed when delivering Owen's. I wanted to roll my eyes and tell him to cut it out, but I chose not to. I had to pick my battles.

We ate in silence, and it wasn't until halfway through my plate when Maximus finally decided to speak up. "It looks like your injuries have healed."

I glanced up, surprised by the broken silence. My fingers went self-consciously to my neck and shoulders, where dozens of vampire bites had covered my skin only days ago. Now it was as if it had never happened.

"They have," I said cautiously.

"I'm glad."

And that was that. Maximus didn't say another word, only finished his breakfast in silence. I exchanged a look with Owen, not sure what to do or say. He shrugged.

Once we were finished, Shira grabbed our plates before any of us could stand to help. She insisted we stay seated, that we had a lot to talk about. She slipped away to load the dishwasher and clean up the counters before I could argue.

"So," Owen started, clearly trying to break the awkward silence. "When do we visit the dragons?"

Maximus glared at the bear shifter. "When the problem with the vampires has been dealt with."

"What?" I asked. "I'm fine now. We should visit Cash and his clan tomorrow."

Maximus shook his head. "No. I won't put you at risk again. You're safer here on pack land."

"So you want me to stay here and twiddle my thumbs for what? A week? Two?"

"However long it takes."

I growled. "We don't even know how they found us. It could have been a coincidence."

Maximus scoffed. "Unlikely."

"I won't just stay here in captivity, Maximus."

Maximus's jaw hardened. "You're not a captive."

"Exactly. Which is why we'll leave tomorrow." I crossed my arms and stared him down.

He sighed. "Ariana..."

"We'll take a different route," I said. "We can bring Shira and some of the other pack members. It'll be fine."

Maximus worked his jaw back and forth. "I don't want you to get hurt again."

I smiled. "I know. But keeping me locked up isn't the answer."

Maximus stared me down for several long moments before finally nodding his approval.

Owen stood abruptly, pulling a cell phone from his pocket. "I'll call Cash." He stepped out of the room, holding the phone to his ear.

Maximus looked at the table, his fist clenched atop it. I reached across and laid my fingers over his knuckles. "It'll be okay."

He took my hand in his and squeezed. He didn't

say anything, only held on as Owen made plans for us to leave tomorrow.

MAXIMUS'S JEEP moved smoothly through the city streets, taking an unnecessarily winding route to wherever we were going. To be sure no vampires got the jump on us this time, we didn't tell anyone what route we were taking. I looked out the back window as we made another sharp turn. Owen's truck barely kept up with us, especially when Maximus made last minute turns seemingly at random.

By the time we stopped in front of a towering skyscraper, it was noon, and the sun blazed off the glass panels of the building, nearly blinding me as I craned my neck to see the top.

"This is it?" I asked.

Maximus grunted something that sounded like yes. He'd had the same standoffish attitude since breakfast yesterday, and it was starting to grate on my nerves.

I glanced into traffic to make sure I had a moment to slip out, then opened the door and made my way around to the sidewalk.

Maximus was at my side in moments. He took my hand, and I squeezed his fingers, hoping to reassure some of his anxiety. Owen pulled up behind us and jumped out with Shira at his side. Together, we made our way to the glass doors and slipped inside.

"You're late," Cash said the moment we were through the door. He sauntered across the luxurious lobby wearing pressed black slacks and a white button down shirt. His grin made me smile in return.

"You can blame Maximus for that," I said.

Maximus shrugged but didn't offer an apology to our host.

"All the same, it's good to have you here." Cash took my arm, weaving it through his and pulling me right from Maximus's grasp. "Let's head up to the penthouse so I can give you the grand tour."

Maximus growled in protest, and it was Cash's turn to ignore him.

Feeling a bit awkward, I could only nod and follow as Cash led the way to the elevators lining the back of the lobby behind a security desk. I marvelled at the marble floors and amazingly high ceilings until we were shoulder to shoulder in a metal box. I realized then that I'd never been in an elevator before.

Once we were all inside, Cash hit a button for the top floor, then keyed in some sort of code on a panel beside the rows upon rows of floor numbers. I barely felt it when the elevator lurched, only a slight airiness in my stomach as we rose. Then the doors chimed and opened. I guess elevators weren't exactly something I'd missed out on during my early years.

"Welcome home, sir," a man said the moment we stepped off the elevator. He wore a black suit and had his dark hair slicked back. His smile was friendly and his eyes warm as he opened an inner door for us to pass through.

"Thank you, Henry," Cash said. "This is Ariana, our new Silver Shifter."

Henry's eyes widened and his mouth dropped open slightly before he could right himself. "Oh, yes. Cash said you would be coming. I didn't realize you'd be so...young."

I wasn't sure what had brought on the sudden awkwardness, but I shook his hand when he offered. I didn't know what to say. I still didn't feel like anything special, though every one of these alphas seemed keen on reminding me that I was.

"You will be a pleasant surprise for many," Cash said. "You're very different from the last Silver Shifter, and it's been so long…"

While I wondered exactly what he meant, Cash led the way through the door to his inner sanctum, a long hall of black and white checkered floor lined by white columns and silver trimmed paintings of people throughout the ages.

"This is my home," Cash said. Instead of gloating at the lavish architecture or glimmering marble floors like I expected, he gazed fondly upon the paintings in gilded frames. "These are portraits of my elders—past dragon alphas."

I followed his gaze to inspect a few, but found it more pleasant to look at his perfectly sculpted face.

Cash led us down the hall to a large living room with white leather furniture, a faux-fur rug and a large fireplace with a pale marble mantle. He didn't linger long, and I followed mechanically. I recognized the signs of wealth when I saw them. I'd known Cash must be wealthy from the way he dressed and his fancy car, but this was beyond what I'd expected. Unlike my former masters, he didn't brag about the things he had. Instead, he drew my eye to his personal possessions: a shelf of ancient tomes, Greek statues, and vases passed down from his grandfather.

We passed a more informal living room and a hallway lined with doors before stopping in a kitchen with dark wood cabinets, stainless steel appliances, and a man with a dark beard chopping vegetables for whatever was stewing in a large pot.

"Peter," Cash greeted.

The chef looked up, his cheeks smudged with flour, and grinned. "Cash, welcome home. How was your trip?"

"It went quite well, thank you."

Peter's gaze slid from his alpha, his blue eyes shining as he met my gaze.

"The Silver Shifter," he whispered with reverence. He stopped what he was doing, dropping his knife on the cutting board before circling the island at the center of the kitchen. "They've finally found you."

I blinked dumbly, again struck by surprise. From what Maximus and the others had told me, the Silver Shifter only appeared once every hundred years, but they didn't specify exactly what one did besides unite the clans. I didn't understand why they looked at me with such joy, or why I was so special to them.

"We have," Cash said when I didn't reply.

Peter clutched my hands and kissed the back of them before he stepped away. "It's good to see another. I only knew the Silver Dragon for a short time, but she was an amazing woman."

"You knew her?" I wanted to learn more about these women who came before me. What were they like? How did they deal with this burden of peacekeeper?

Peter nodded. "I did, though I was young. She had a kind soul and a beautiful smile."

"I wish I'd known her," I said.

Peter smiled. "Of course, that's impossible. Only one can live at once."

I smiled, not sure what to say.

"Peter, could you whip up something for my guests?" Cash asked.

"Of course." The chef grinned and his eyes lit up. "I'll get started right away."

"Thank you." Cash nodded and led the way out of the kitchen.

I watched him as he led us through a few more rooms, surprised by how much more at ease he seemed in his own element. Not only that, but he held himself differently. He was more commanding but had a gentleness to the way he asked for things. He didn't look down on anyone who worked for him. In fact, it seemed like they were all great friends.

Something stirred inside of me as we continued, and my wolf began her typical mantra of *mine, mine, mine.*

Was Cash mine, too? This was getting just plain ridiculous. Was my wolf going to claim every alpha she met?

"Sir," someone called from the end of the hall, stopping my train of thought.

Cash looked back over his shoulder. "Henry. What is it?"

The doorman slowed to a stop in front of them. "A messenger from the council has arrived. They want to meet with you and the Silver Shifter."

Cash sighed. "Already?"

Henry nodded. "It seems so."

Cash looked at me, a smile twisting his lips. "It seems we'll have to finish our tour later. The Dragon Council aren't a patient lot."

## 14

## CASH

Ariana's small hand tightened on my arm. "Dragon Council?"

I sighed internally. I always hated dealing with the elder council. They were all stodgy old men and women, the very oldest of dragons. They constantly referred to the old ways and hated anything new presented to them. In my early days as alpha, they'd tested me constantly, not liking my new ideas on how to do things, especially when it came to strengthening the bond between the New York Clans.

"Yes, though I'm sorry we haven't gotten more time together first," I said. "It's tradition for the Silver Shifter to meet the Dragon Council. Don't worry, we won't stay long."

"The Dragon Council?" Maximus stepped closer. "You aren't taking her there alone."

Ariana regarded me with a raised eyebrow and

pursed lips. I couldn't stop my gaze from lingering on them, so pink and perfect and kissable.

*Stop*, I commanded myself. Ariana wasn't my mate, no matter what my dragon said.

As if to prove me wrong, my dragon hissed, *Mine*.

Ever since I'd laid eyes on this frail girl tumbling off a cliff, something inside me had shifted. Though I hadn't known who she was until we'd landed, the sight of her made my blood burn and my breath catch. I wanted her like I'd never wanted anything else before.

And she belonged to someone else.

"I'll be fine, Maximus," Ariana said. Though her tone was soft, I could see the tiny twitch in her cheek. She was getting tired of Maximus's overprotectiveness.

My dragon rumbled. He didn't like Maximus, either. He was too alpha, always trying to be the top dog. I smirked at the turn of phrase. At least Owen wasn't like the wolves. He was far easier to get along with. Out of all of them, I'd been closest to Jett, though. Once, we'd been real friends.

"It'll only be for thirty minutes tops," I said to Ariana, shaking my gloomy thoughts away.

Maximus's gaze flashed yellow as he looked between us. "Fine. Thirty minutes. Any more and I don't care what your laws say, I will break up your meeting."

I couldn't really blame Maximus. If Ariana was mine, I would never let her out of my sight. Besides, I didn't want to spend any more time than that with the council. In fact, I was hoping we'd be in and out in ten minutes. Maybe then I could steal some more time away with Ariana.

I froze, stopping my train of thought right there. My dragon was starting to get to me with all of his talk of Ariana being ours.

"Understood," I said.

Ariana looked at the others once more before allowing me to lead her back to the elevator. She stayed quiet, her hand tight on my arm until the doors to the elevator shut behind us.

"What does your council want with me?" she asked.

I smiled. "Nothing bad, I assure you."

She worried her lip between her teeth, and it was possibly the most adorable thing I'd ever seen. My fingers brushed her cheek lightly, pushing a loose strand of hair behind her ear. She froze.

I stilled too, not having realized what I was doing. Flirting with the Silver Shifter was one thing, but I had to keep my head. I cleared my throat and dropped my hand to pat the back of her fingers. "They're harmless, I promise. They're only a bunch of stodgy old fools."

Ariana snorted.

We didn't have to go far to meet with the council. We descended a few levels to the council's private floor. I think they took the floor closest to me just so they could bother me with every inane thing imaginable.

The elevator slowed to a stop, and the doors chimed open. I stepped out, leading Ariana down a hall of dark marble floors and gold trimmed walls. Paintings of past alphas were placed every few feet, old sconces between them. The council liked their theatrics as much as they liked their money. As dragons, we all found our own vices to hoard. Mine happened to be nice cars and the latest tech toys, while the council seemed intent on finding every piece of dragon history possible to darken our halls.

We stopped outside a set of oak doors, and I glanced down at Ariana to make sure she was ready. Her eyebrows were furrowed as she stared intently at the door. She was so small, and yet so mighty. After all she'd been through her spirit was still so alive, so defiant. I wouldn't expect anything less from the Silver Shifter.

I opened the door and motioned Ariana in first. She hesitated before letting my arm go and stepping inside. I followed close behind, closing the door before I turned to face a conference table with eight dragon shifters surrounding it.

Two chairs remained open for us, side by side closest to the door. At least it'd make for an easy escape should they take up too much of my time *again*.

"Cash. Silver Shifter. Welcome." Virion, the oldest of the dragons and leader of the council, bowed his head in greeting. Though his hair was whiter than snow and his face creased with a thousand wrinkles, he still had a spark in his eyes. I knew that spark all too well—and how quickly it could grow into an inferno.

"Council," I greeted before pulling out Ariana's chair and urging her to sit. Once she did, I pushed her chair in and took my own.

My heartbeat sped up, and my palms began to sweat. I really didn't enjoy being in their presence. Despite my words to Arianna, they had enough power to intimidate me. If I had my way, I'd abolish the council altogether, but the my clan would riot at such a break in tradition or I'd have done it already.

"What a beauty," another councilman remarked. Anton didn't leer at Ariana, but instead inspected her silver hair with fondness. Every member of the council had known my mother, the Silver Dragon.

"Thank you." Ariana dipped her head slightly before straightening to return their examination.

"She's very small," councilwoman Genevieve huffed. "I hope you're having Peter make her something to eat."

I chuckled. "Of course."

"I hear you had some trouble last week," Laurence said, the youngest councilman and the one I most despised. Even now, his harsh black gaze scanned Ariana, giving her a look that made me want to tear his eyes from his head.

"Vampires," I said, not wanting to elaborate further. They didn't need to know specifics.

"You've both recovered well?" Virion asked.

"Yes," I said.

Ariana touched her neck as if recalling her vampire bites. They were long gone now, but I'd never forget them either. My fists clenched at the memory of blood coating her pale skin. My dragon rumbled inside me, and I took a deep breath.

"Who ever heard of vampires attacking out in the open like this?" Laurence huffed. "It's blasphemous to attack the Silver Shifter."

"They clearly didn't know who she was," Anton said.

"That, or their queen is up to something," Laurence said.

I shook my head. "We shouldn't speculate. I have men on it. We'll find out what happened."

"Good, good." Virion nodded. "Now, Miss Ariana, you were born a wolf, yes?"

Ariana shifted uncomfortably. "Yes."

"But you were born outside the New York pack?"

Again, Ariana confirmed.

"And is it true you were a slave to a warlock?" Laurence asked.

The entire council went silent.

"That's an awful way of putting it," I snapped. I didn't like how Laurence was treating Ariana, and we'd barely been in the room for a minute.

"But it is true, isn't it?" He inclined his head and eyed Ariana like a predator.

Ariana set her jaw. "Yes."

"And you were found acting like a savage animal?" Laurence asked.

I stood, hands slamming against the table. "That's enough."

"Calm yourself, Cash," Virion said, though he glared at Laurence. "That *is* quite enough, Laurence. We already know these things."

"I simply wanted to confirm," Laurence said.

I barely held back a growl as I lowered myself back into my seat. "Are these the kind of things you really want to ask the Silver Shifter?"

"No," Anton said. He too glared at his fellow councilman.

"In what order are you visiting the clans?" Genevieve asked, trying to clear the tension left in the air.

I took a deep breath. "Dragons, Bears, and then the Panthers."

Anton raised an eyebrow at that. He'd been a mentor to me after my father died and I took over, and even before that. He knew my history with Jett.

"And what are your plans after that?" Virion asked. "The Silver Dragon foretold the next Silver Shifter would bring the four clans together. How do you intend to make this happen?"

"Yes, we'd love to hear it," Laurence added.

Ariana paled and her lips parted. She had no more idea than I did. The clans had been at war on and off for centuries, and tensions had only gotten worse since the death of the Silver Dragon.

"Her plans will be under wraps until she assesses the state of the clans," I said. I couldn't leave Ariana alone in this. She'd hardly been with us for more than a couple of weeks. She had no idea how high tensions were.

Ariana gave me a grateful look, and my dragon purred. Actually *purred*. My chest heated, and I had to take a deep breath to calm myself and my dragon.

"A smart move," Anton said. He inspected Ariana and nodded his approval. "We look forward to your thoughts after you've finished your visits."

Ariana smiled stiffly and squeezed my hand under the table. Heat shot up my arm, and I entwined my fingers with hers.

*Miiine*, my dragon hissed.

My jaw hardened and my heart raced. I couldn't help but wish my dragon was right, that somehow, some way, Ariana was ours.

"I'm sure your ideas will change the world," Laurence said with a smirk.

I could taste fire suddenly, and I knew then that if I didn't get out of this damn room, I'd burn it to the ground.

"We'll take our leave now." I stood, gripping

Ariana's hand firmly. She gave me a quizzical look, but I couldn't take my gaze off Laurence.

"Enjoy your visit," Genevieve said.

Ariana pulled on my arm, and I was forced to break my staredown with Laurence. She smiled, and all the anger building inside me fled.

"Thank you," she told the council.

Upon the great Dragon God's grace, we were allowed to leave, and as soon as the door shut behind us, weight lifted from my shoulders.

"That was... interesting," Ariana said.

I shook my head. "That's one word for it."

Ariana grinned, and so did I. "Let's finish the tour, shall we?"

She nodded, and I led the way back to the elevator, grateful when the doors closed on my least favorite floor in the entire building.

## 15

## ARIANA

Instead of stopping on the floor we had earlier, Cash stopped the elevator on the floor below it.

"What now?" I asked, narrowing my eyes at Cash. "Don't tell me I have to pass another test, because I'm not sure I passed the last one."

"That wasn't a test," he said, his hand landing on my lower back as he guided me out of the elevator. "And you were great, Ari. Better than they deserved."

"Then what?" I asked as he nudged me towards a door at the end of the hall.

"You'll see," he answered, a wicked grin on his face.

"Why do I feel like I'm walking into a trap?" I didn't feel unsafe, though. Cash had defended me with his life when the vampires attacked. I just wasn't sure if I was the kind of person who liked surprises.

"Don't you trust me?" Cash asked, his eyes

sparkling with humor as he pushed open the door. I was greeted by a set of smooth granite stairs.

"I'm not sure," I said, giving him some side-eye as I stepped into the stairway with him.

"I just thought you might need a break after all of those people," he said. "Maximus and Owen will be waiting for us at the elevator. If we go up this way, I can show you around in peace."

My wolf stirred at the thought of having Cash all to myself. Besides the time he'd caught me falling and flown me back to Maximus's, I'd never been alone with him.

*Mine*, she whispered in the back of my head.

*That's not possible*, I thought back to her. I already had, somehow, two mates. Three just seemed selfish.

"That sounds perfect," I said. After being paraded around the house meeting all of Cash's servants, and then being put on the spot and having to stand up in front of all those intimidating dragons, I was ready for something less stressful.

Gripping my hand, Cash started up the stairs with me one step behind. I admired the hard plains of his back as we climbed, the muscles subtly apparent under his dress shirt. My wolf must be confused. Sure, Cash had flirted with me a little, and he'd protected me. But that was because I was the Silver Shifter, not because he felt anything more for me. I was here on official business, for completely political reasons. He'd introduced me to the Dragon Council, not his mother.

Still, warmth climbed my arm from our linked hands, growing with each step we took. He pushed open a door and gave me that arrogant, irresistible smile as we stepped back into his opulent condo. We were in a short hallway with heavy rugs lain along the hardwood floor. For a second, I hesitated halfway through the door. Our eyes met, and the warmth that had built inside me pulsed hotter. The smile dropped from Cash's full lips, and his fingertips grazed my waist.

"Ariana," he said, his voice low in his throat, his eyes dropping to my mouth. My name sounded delicious on his tongue, his accent caressing each syllable sensually.

"Yes?"

*Mine*, my wolf growled, more insistent this time. She was salivating to claim him.

"Do you want to see the bedrooms?" he asked.

I gulped at the thought. On the one hand, hell yes, I wanted to see his bedroom. On the other hand... My two mates were standing on the other side of the condo, waiting for me outside a silent elevator.

My wolf growled, this time at me, irritated by my resistance to her claims.

Cash's hand slid from my waist to my lower back, and he urged me through the door and into the hallway. "These are my guest rooms," he said, opening a door on either side of the hallway. Each was large but furnished with personal items that he explained briefly—a painting of his ancestral lands, a bust of an alpha somewhere in his lineage, and figures of East Indian gods carved from marble and ebony.

"And my bedroom," he said, his voice dropping even lower.

I'd never seen this side of Cash, all the usual teasing gone. He was both relaxed and intense, and I didn't know exactly how to react. He opened the door and stepped inside, and after a brief hesitation, I stepped in after him. The luxurious softness of the carpet absorbed our footsteps as he slid his arm around my waist and led me around the spacious room. It was similar to the rest of the place but both larger and more luxurious, with so many of his trinkets and decorations that it was one item short of being cluttered.

A huge bed dominated the room, the mahogany frame and brocade spread making it look more like a king's bed than an alpha's. But then again, I guessed being an alpha was pretty much the same thing. We stood staring at it for a minute, heat coursing between us.

"That's a big bed," I said after a pause.

"There's a lot to do in it," he said, his throaty voice caressing my nerve endings.

The animal pull I had towards him was blocked by my human brain as it latched onto those words. A lot to do in the bed. He'd probably done lots in it, too, and with lots of women. Between his looks and his money,

I could be pretty certain he never spent a single night alone.

And there was my wolf again, growling with fierce jealousy.

"I'm sure there is," I said, pulling away from him a bit.

Cash smirked at me. "Want to see the rest of the place?"

"How much more is there?"

"If you're not too tired, there's just one more thing I want to show you."

"What's that?" I asked, raising an eyebrow.

"You'll see."

I tried not to let my irritation show as I followed him back to the stairs. We took them down to the next floor, then climbed back into the elevator. I imagined Maximus up there, watching the numbers rise, then stop, then fall again, without returning to his floor. He was probably going nuts up there. Knowing him, he'd already come looking for me and was freaking out that he hadn't found me. Part of me felt guilty, but another part thought, good. He had to know that I couldn't stand his constant hovering. I appreciated his protectiveness, but I needed freedom, too.

We stepped out of the elevator into an enormous garage lit by bright overhead lights that glinted off the glossy hoods of a dozen sleek, luxury cars.

Cash hurried into the garage, nearly skipping, and

threw his arms wide. "Meet my babies," he said with a grin.

"Do they have names?" I asked, unable to keep from smiling back at him.

"Would you expect anything less?" he said, running his fingertips lovingly over the gleaming surface of a vintage yellow Mustang. "This is Sally, named for the Al Green song."

"What about this one?" I asked, my hand hovering above a cherry-red Corvette.

"That's Prince," he said, crossing his arms and smiling proudly. "My little red Corvette."

I couldn't help but admire the way his biceps bulged when he stood like that, lord of all these sexy machines.

"Can we ride in one?" I asked.

"I thought you'd never ask," he said, his smile growing broader. He darted past me, giving my backside a playful swat on the way.

I jumped and let out a little squawk. "Hey!"

Cash shot me a grin over his shoulder as he lay his palm on a glass case. "Pick one."

I pointed at a gleaming black Ferrari, something I'd only ever seen on TV.

A red light came on inside the case, and a second later, it popped open. He pocketed one of the keys from inside and strode toward me, his face lit with excitement. It was contagious, and I found myself running over and sliding into the passenger seat before he'd reached the car. It was so low to the ground I had to duck to get in, but my legs had plenty of room. I lay back on the reclined leather seat, running my fingers along the supple material.

"You're not going to let me be a gentleman?" Cash asked, arching an eyebrow as he slid in behind the wheel. "I would have gotten your door."

"Maybe tomorrow," I said. "After meeting your council, I think I've had enough of gentlemen for today."

Cash laughed and revved the engine. "I'll keep that in mind."

As the garage door lifted, he maneuvered the little car between the others and out through the gate that lifted to let us onto the street.

"Maximus is going to kill me," I said, but I was already glad I'd gotten away. Just for a while, I wanted a taste of freedom, a moment to make my own choices and not be treated like something precious and fragile.

"You're perfectly safe with me," Cash said with a smug smile. "Probably safer than with him. A dragon can take a wolf any day."

"True," I said slowly. Besides, sneaking out in a fast car with a sexy man seemed like the perfect way to let Maximus know that he couldn't make every decision for me. I'd told him, but it hadn't sunk in. Maybe I had to show him. I knew he was doing it with good intentions, but it was smothering my spirit.

"How fast does this thing go?" I asked, running my hands along the dash.

Cash shot me a surprised look. "Really?"

"Really what?"

"You want to find out how fast it goes?"

"You don't know?" I blinked in surprise.

"Oh, I know," he said. "But it's more fun to see for yourself."

"I guess for a guy who flies, this isn't very exciting."

"If you don't want to, that's okay. I understand. It's not for everyone."

I sat up straighter and adjusted the seat back. "You can't dangle that in front of me and then take it away," I protested. "I can't fly. I'm a wolf. So show me how fast it goes."

A slow smile spread across his lips. "How fast do you want to go?"

I bit at the corner of my lip for a second while I thought. "I don't know," I said. "I've never been in a car like this."

"Buckle up," he said. "And get ready for Maximus to kill us both."

The car slid forward almost silently on the street, and at first, I could barely tell we were going fast. The engine began to purr as we streaked forward, the buildings blurring past.

"What if we get pulled over?" I asked as he wove in and out of traffic.

"Don't worry about it," he said. "There's a dragon on the force who takes care of me."

We shot past a handful of cars and suddenly, we were on a bridge. The city sparkled around us, but for a second, I felt like we were airborne as we shot across. My heart leapt, and I turned to Cash. "Can we put the top down?"

He laughed and shook his head. "Let's not get ahead of ourselves."

Soon, we were out of the city, and the traffic became more scarce.

"Now?" I asked. "Come on, I've never ridden in a convertible. Where's the fun if we don't have the top down?"

Cash laughed and pushed a button, and the top retracted above us. The cool night air rushed past, and I laughed, grabbing at my silver hair as it whipped around me. Cash pushed the Ferrari faster, zipping along the road, the tires hugging the turns.

"This fast enough for you?" he said, yelling so I could hear him over the growl of the engine and the wind. I could feel the vibration of the motor through me, charging my blood.

"Not even close!" I yelled as we shot over a small hill and dipped again. My stomach bottomed out and a little whoop escaped my lips.

Cash laughed, shifting gears and pushing us faster.

I felt a sudden tug, and realized it was Maximus

contacting me through our pack bond. If he could see me now...

Cash was right. He'd kill us both.

But I wasn't going to let that stop me. I pushed down my shield, letting Maximus in. I didn't know exactly what he could and couldn't see through the bond, but at least he would know I was safe and happy right now. Letting him in was an unexpected relief, too. I suddenly felt as if he was with me, another of my mates riding along beside me. In a way, he was here. I let him all the way in, welcoming him. I only wished Owen could be here, too.

The car growled as it climbed a steeper hill. I hugged my arms around myself, my heart pounding with anticipation. When we crested the hill, it was even better than I'd expected.

The road lay before us, the yellow lines winding down the long slope below. Cash shot me a grin, and we began to drop. My stomach lurched again, and I threw up my hands and whooped like I was on a roller coaster as we gained speed, dropping faster and faster until I felt like we really were flying. We zipped around a curve, coming up on a pair of tail lights so fast I let out a little scream.

Cash steered around them, but a pair of headlights flashed into our eyes. I gripped the dash, fear and exhilaration jolting through me. We veered back into our lane, streaking by the other car as it blared its horn. Laughter burst from me and filled the night. I'd never felt so alive, so invincible. So free.

"Faster," I shouted, reaching over and grabbing Cash's knee, pressing it down on the gas.

He was laughing, too, the sound beautiful as it mixed with mine. Inside, my wolf was baying her approval. For the first time I could remember, even if it was only for this moment, no one was asking anything of me. I didn't have to be the best fighter. I didn't have to be someone's savior. I didn't have to be afraid of the next moment.

And then suddenly, we were flying around a curve that was so sharp the tires were spinning. The car was spinning. Cash swore and twisted the wheel, pushing into the turn. We shot across a stretch of grass and through a wire fence. The Ferrari slid to a stop, and for a second, the night was silent around us. Then I started laughing.

"It's not funny," Cash growled. "This is my favorite car."

I couldn't stop, though. Adrenaline barreled through me. Cash jumped out of the car, and a second later, he was opening my door and pulling me out.

"You're crazy, you know that?" he said.

My wolf was alive, writhing inside my skin, howling to be released. She wanted to run free and wild, but this was my time. *My* night to run free and wild.

I threw my arms around his neck and pressed my lips to his, hard. Cash grabbed my face between both hands, crushing his mouth to mine. He pushed me back against the car, his hips grinding into mine. I could feel his hardness biting into me, and in that moment, I needed him like I'd never needed anything in my life.

I wrapped my legs around his waist, and his arm circled my back, crushing my hips down on his. My wolf howled for more, shuddering through my body, fighting for control.

*No*, I told her. *My turn.*

I grabbed the front of his shirt with both hands and yanked it open, barely hearing the buttons plinking against the metal hood. His brown skin shone in the moonlight, his nipples instantly hardening when the chill in the air hit them. My hands greedily reached for him, and I gasped at the infernal heat of his skin. My wolf snarled for more, and I raked my nails down the ridges of muscle that made up his abdomen, eliciting a growl of pain from him.

"Is that how you want to play?" Cash growled. He bent, slamming me down on the hood of the car.

A cry escaped me as he yanked me to the edge of the hood, and I pushed up onto my elbow, my other arm circling his neck. I bit at his lip, my wolf raging for me to claim him. He was mine, mine, *mine*.

He yanked at my pants, sliding the zipper down and slipping his hand inside. I arched up, opening my thighs and welcoming his long fingers as they drove into me.

"My god, you're already wet," he moaned into my neck, his lips burning across my skin. He pushed my jeans down, the cold air of the night sending a chill racing through my feverish body as he stepped between my thighs. The heat of the hood beneath me and the cold of the cool night swallowed me, and something inside me soared up, like I was more than a wolf, like I could fly alongside him, my third mate.

Suddenly, the head of his cock was pressing against my wetness. I gasped, brought back to the present moment, in the field, on the hood of his car, with a dragon alpha bending over me. I had not claimed him as my mate, but he was about to claim me in a different way, a way no one else ever had. I opened my mouth to tell him, but he spoke first.

"Ariana," Cash growled. "You're mine."

"Is your dragon confused, too?" I asked, my legs trembling as I stared up at his chiseled features, barely visible in the night. It was enough. Enough to see all the fire and need in his eyes that matched my own.

"Hell no," he said. "My dragon knows what's his when he sees it."

He thrust forward, forcing his cock inside me. I cried out, shocked by the sudden pain and the heat of him tearing into me. He answered with a cry of his own, mistaking my pain for something else. I hadn't had time to tell him I'd never done this before, and now it was too late. Now I had.

He ground himself deeper until our hips connected, and then he paused, breathing hard. "I'll wait," he said, his lips skimming along my throat, his hips locked against mine but not moving.

I was still gasping with pain, but the longer he stayed there, his cock filling me but infuriatingly motionless inside me, the harder it became to stay still. My wolf was roaring with a furious need to claim this man, and my body was in agreement. As the pain subsided, frustration took its place. I wanted him to move. To go fast and wild like we had in the car. I squirmed under him, my nails raking across his back.

"Now," I said. "I'm ready."

Cash sucked in a breath and drew his hips back, then drove forward, filling me again. I gasped in pain, but this time, there was pleasure along with it. Gripping my thighs, he pulled my hips to the edge of the car and began thrusting into me rhythmically. I pushed up on my elbows, watching him, watching our bodies together. His muscles contracted and expanded, outlined beautifully in the moonlight, his hips flexing as he gave me every inch of him until I couldn't bear it.

I lifted my arm, clamping it around his neck. "Let me claim you, too," I said, snapping my teeth at his lip and catching it on the first try. He grunted in pain, but I didn't release him. Instead, I bit down harder. The harder I bit, the harder he drove into me, growling as he slammed me against the hot metal of the car. When I tasted his blood, I released his lip, but he caught mine between his teeth before I could pull back.

He held my hips and pushed all the way in, grinding himself deeper into me. I winced as he reached my depths, but he held me pinned, his cock throbbing deep inside me. He gave my lip a quick, sharp bite, and sucked. The sensation shot straight to my clit, and I gasped, my walls clenching around him. He groaned with pleasure, the vibration spreading through my whole body. I arched up, crushing my clit against his pelvic bone. He groaned again, sucking harder, and suddenly, the shimmering waves of pleasure I'd felt with Owen came crashing over me, spreading through my body and lifting me up.

Cash drew back, resting his hands on the car beside me, and thrust into me one final time. Pleasure rocketed through my body and I cried out as his come flooded into me as hot as spurts of lava. For a minute neither of us moved, and the heat inside me began to cool. At last, Cash pushed himself upright and wiped his mouth.

"Remember when we said Maximus was going to kill us?" he asked, bending to pull up his pants and button them.

While he was occupied, I hopped off the hood of the car, trying not to show how much it hurt to sit up.

"Let me worry about Maximus," I said. "Tonight isn't about him."

"Damn right," Cash said, pulling me close and pressing his lips to mine. "It's about us. You're my mate now, Ari." He cradled my cheek in one hand, his palm warm against my skin.

"About that," I said.

"What about it?" he asked, drawing back a little. "We claimed each other. Our blood mingled. There can be no doubt in anyone's mind, no matter what Maximus would prefer."

That was true—just not the whole truth. I knew that Maximus would definitely prefer to be my only mate. And yet, he wasn't.

Inside me, my wolf was lounging happily, satisfied at last. Finally, I understood what she'd been trying to tell me all along. I had accepted Maximus first because it was obvious and expected that the Silver Shifter was the mate of the alpha of her clan. But it was more complicated than that.

Because I wasn't simply supposed to be with the expected alpha, or even to choose one of the other alphas as a mate. I was supposed to choose all four.

## 16

## ARIANA

I woke up to sunlight shining on my face. With a groan, I untangled myself from Cash. I could use a serious dose of mouthwash. Or a whole bottle.

It took me a second to realize where we were—curled up on the leather seat of his Ferrari in the middle of a field. And it was daylight.

*Fuck.*

"Cash," I said, shaking his shoulder. "We need to get back. They're going to kill us."

He opened his eyes and smiled, his dark hair mussed from sleep. He reached for me, but I swatted his hand away.

"Seriously, we have to get back," I said. I could feel Maximus's distress through our pack bond, and worse, his despair.

"If they're going to kill us anyway…" Cash said with a grin.

"I mean it," I said, taking his hand and giving him a pleading look. "Take me back."

As Cash climbed in the driver's seat, I closed my eyes and opened my mind to Maximus.

*I'm okay. I'm on my way back.*

"He would have come and found you if you were in danger," Cash said. "He knew you were okay."

"I know," I said. "But…"

I couldn't explain to Cash how much it hurt to hurt my alpha. His pain was my pain, and knowing I'd caused it only made it worse. I was pretty sure my wolf was right about my mates. Cash was my mate, and so was Owen, and even Jett, who I barely knew. But Maximus was my alpha.

We were wolves, and even though my wolf had somehow been destined for four mates, I was still part of Maximus's pack. He was the only one of them who could command me, thank heaven for small favors. I didn't even like him doing it, and I couldn't imagine being under the command of all four of them.

When we got back to the city, Cash turned to me.

"Let me handle Maximus," he said. "This is between us."

"This? You mean me." I narrowed my eyes.

He quirked an eyebrow. "I guess I do mean you."

"So how about you let me handle Maximus?"

"I have more experience in that department."

"True," I said. "But somehow I think I can diffuse the situation in ways you can't."

He shot me a frown. "What ways?"

I sighed. "Let me talk to him, okay? And then you can do your little dance for dominance."

"Little dance?" he asked with a smirk. "Like a cha-cha?"

"Whatever you want to call it," I said, turning to the window to hide my smile. I was glad Cash was acting so normal, like nothing had happened. Not awkward, like we were avoiding the topic of the night before, but like nothing had changed. As distracted as I was, I didn't think I was up for heavy declarations. Still, he was so normal it made me wonder again how often he did this. It might have been just another night of crazy sex for him. For me, it had been a night I'd never forget as long as I lived.

When we got out of the car, I was reminded of it with every step I took. I was really fucking sore. It hurt worse now than it had the night before.

When we got in the elevator, Cash pulled me close and gave me a lingering kiss. My heart was already racing, and the kiss just made it worse.

"Don't tell me you're doubting what happened last night," he said.

"No," I said. "But...can we talk about this later?"

I could only handle one mate at a time right now. My head was still spinning with the realization that I had four. *Four.* How the hell was I going to juggle them all? Although from the waves of fury coming through the pack bond from Maximus, I thought he might just kill the other three and take care of the problem once and for all.

And then we'd have an all-out war on our hands.

Shit. Wasn't I supposed to smooth things over between the clans and make peace? How the hell was getting tangled up with all four of the alphas going to accomplish that?

The second we stepped out of the elevator, Maximus launched himself out of his chair and grabbed my arm, pulling me to him. "You're going to pay for this," he growled over my shoulder at Cash, his voice murderously calm.

"Maximus, it's okay," I said, gripping his upper arms with both hands. "He didn't do anything wrong. He didn't hurt me."

"I know that," Maximus said, still staring at Cash, his eyes flashing molten gold. "I would have found you and killed him."

"Trust me, I didn't do anything to Ari that she didn't want," Cash said with an easy grin.

Maximus lunged forward, but when I blocked his way, he let me stop him. I pushed him back, flattening my hands against his ripped chest. His muscles were tensed so hard they shook under my palms.

"He's right," I said, swallowing hard.

Maximus took a deep breath, his nostrils flaring. Pain rippled through our bond. "I'm glad you're back, Silver Shifter," he said. Then he turned and stalked off.

My throat tightened, though I knew from my years in the cages that crying did nothing but show people how to hurt you more. But Max... He was my mate. And he hadn't looked at me once, not even when he'd spoken to me. I couldn't stop the ache of tears at the back of my eyes, but I refused to shed them. I wanted to collapse into the boxy leather chair he'd set up to watch the elevator and wait for our return, but I couldn't leave things like this for even one more minute. The gulf that had opened between us was unbearable.

Cash caught my arm and pulled me in. "We can break the news to him together."

"No," I said. "I need to do this."

He shrugged and released me. "If you need me, I'll be in the garage. The Ferrari's not used to jumping ditches. I better make sure she's okay."

I turned and squared my shoulders, taking a deep breath before starting down the hall. I felt like I was marching down death row. If this was how the whole Silver Shifter thing was going to be, I wasn't sure I wanted any part of it. Smoothing things over between alphas was not fun. And how was I supposed to know how? Making peace was the exact opposite of what I'd been doing for the past decade.

I stopped at the door to the guest room where Maximus had gone. "Maximus?" I said. "Can I come in?"

Nothing.

"Seriously?" I said. "I know you're there. I can feel you through our bond, too. Don't you think this is a little immature?"

The door swung open and Maximus grabbed me and pulled me inside, shutting the door hard behind me. "Immature?" he growled. "You took off without telling anyone, in a city where we were attacked just a week ago. We barely fended off a vampire attack with all three of us there to protect you. And then you come waltzing back in and expect me to pretend nothing is wrong?"

He was breathing hard, his eyes flashing gold at me like a warning. My own wolf leapt to the surface, ready to fight back. "I'm not asking you to pretend," I said, determined to keep my cool and be the mature one for once. "I'm sorry I worried you."

"Are you?" he demanded. "Because I didn't feel much remorse coming through. You did whatever you wanted, laughing at our concern while you ran straight into the face of danger."

Forget keeping my cool. I wasn't going to let him talk to me that way.

"Well, excuse me for doing something I wanted for once in my life," I shot back. "I haven't gotten a chance to be selfish for one fucking minute in the last decade. I think I'm a little overdue."

"This isn't just about you," Maximus roared. "You need to think about the pack. About all four clans.

You're not just a pit fighter anymore. You're the Silver Shifter."

"I never asked to be your fucking savior," I yelled back at him. My wolf was raging to get out, to rip him apart for accosting me.

"You don't get to make that choice," Maximus said, his voice low and even. "You already are."

His words sent a bucket of ice water cascading over me, instantly cooling my anger and sobering me to the reality I faced. I'd run off and had fun last night, but I couldn't escape this. Like it or not, I was their damn Silver Shifter.

"Well," I said after a long moment of silence. "I'm sorry I put your Silver Shifter in danger and made you worry about your future alliances."

"I wasn't worried about our future alliances," Maximus said. "I was worried about you."

We stood there staring each other down for a minute.

"You slept with him," he said, his eyes hard.

I didn't know what else to say, so I just nodded. "Yes."

"You're *my* mate," he growled, his voice harsh with anger and pain. He grabbed my shoulders and glared at me like he wanted to shake me. "Do you hear that? You're not his to touch, to claim, to take. You're *mine*." His mouth crashed down against mine so hard I could feel my teeth cutting into my lip.

My wolf growled with pleasure, and my arms

circled Maximus's body. His neck arched as he leaned down to kiss me, his hands pressing into the small of my back, drawing me hard against him. But when I opened my mouth for his tongue, he pulled away. His eyes searched mine, the anguish clear in his gaze.

"If you know I'm your mate, if you feel this way about me, then how could you—" His voice broke, and he stopped speaking, his eyes cutting away from mine.

I took his chin in my hand and turned his face back to me. "Because," I said. "He's my mate, too. I let you into my head, Maximus. You know that."

"It's not possible."

"I know," I said. "But it's true."

"Cash knows better than that," Maximus said through clenched teeth, his hands curling into fists. "And you... No matter how new you are to this, you know what it means to be someone's mate. It's instinctual. I would *never* go behind your back with another woman."

Tears sprang to my eyes, pain cutting through me at his words. I'd expected his anger, but his hurt was harder to bear.

"I didn't go behind your back," I said.

"No," he said. "You rubbed it in my face."

"I didn't," I said, swiping at a tear.

"You shut me out all week, but when you're with him, you let me in. What do you call that?"

I gulped past the ache clenching my throat shut. "I wanted you to know why."

"There's nothing to excuse what you've done, Ariana."

"You don't understand," I said, a tear trickling down my cheek.

Maximus swallowed hard a few times, and then he stepped over and pulled me into his arms. His chest was tense, his body stiff even as he held me. I fisted my hand in his shirt, choking on my sobs.

"You're right," Maximus said, his voice softer now. "I don't understand. But I'm your mate, and what you did doesn't change that. Nothing can."

"There's no way out of it," I said, lifting my teary face. "Right? Once your wolf chooses a mate, it doesn't matter what they do. You're bound together for life."

"Yes," Maximus said. The sadness in his voice tore at my heart. Did he want a different mate? Did he wish his wolf had chosen someone else?

"Well, if you want the truth, it hurt like hell," I said. "I hope you're happy."

Maximus's eyes flashed yellow. "He hurt you? I'm going to fucking kill him."

"No," I cried, grabbing his arm. I could feel a vein in his upper arm pulsing hard and fast with anger. "I—I wanted him to."

"You wanted him to hurt you?" Maximus asked, his fiery eyes fixing on my face.

"I wanted him to—no, *I* wanted to claim *him*. My wolf claimed him as her mate, Maximus. Like you said, it can't be undone."

"That can't be," he said, his voice choked. For a second, I thought he'd cry, too.

"She's been telling me all along," I whispered. "But I was confused by your stupid Silver Shifter traditions, and I haven't been listening to her. But Maximus, I'm not just *your* mate."

"What are you saying, Ari?" he asked, and I could feel the hurt twisting his heart.

Fresh tears sprang to my eyes. Seeing him in pain was almost enough to make me take it back. Almost. But I couldn't deny my true feelings, not even for one of my mates.

"I'm saying I have two mates. I don't know how it's possible, but my wolf hasn't released her claim on you. I have more than one mate, that's all." I tried to say it gently to placate him, but Maximus's shoulders tensed, letting me know my easy tone had not softened him.

He stared down at me like he didn't trust me, like I was a stranger. "Is that all?"

"No," I admitted, suddenly trembling under his gaze. "Owen is my mate, too. And...maybe Jett, too. I don't know for sure, but my wolf wanted to claim you all when you were together that day."

He gulped, cords of muscle standing out in his neck. "Anyone else?"

I shook my head, tears rising in my eyes again. "No."

"So I get one fourth of a mate."

"No," I said, shaking my head hard. "Claiming them doesn't make my claim to you any less strong. In fact, it seems to be getting stronger. I feel things for you that I didn't when it was just us. I'm your mate, Maximus. Never doubt that."

"I never have." His face softened, and he reached up and stroked my hair behind my ears and then cupped my face between his hands. He ran his thumbs across my cheeks, drying my tears.

"And you're my mate, Maximus," I said, raising my eyes to his. "My first mate."

He let out a soft snort as if he didn't believe me.

I clutched his forearms, but he dropped his hands to my shoulders and simply stared into my eyes, dropping his shield so I could feel the turmoil of emotion rolling through him like storm-tossed waves.

"Are you mad at me?" I whispered, my heart twisting with anguish.

"No," he said quietly. "I'm hurt that you chose Cash to be your first."

His honestly punched straight at my heart. I squeezed my eyes closed, another tear leaking from under my lid and sliding down my cheek. "I didn't. It just happened. You are all equal to my wolf. She doesn't care about first or second. She just wants. She's an animal."

"So am I. But you don't see me losing control and —" His voice broke, and he took a breath before finishing. "Hurting you."

"Then show me what it's like when it doesn't hurt," I said, stepping into his arms. "I claimed you first, Maximus. Now claim me."

A primal, animal growl rumbled somewhere deep in his throat, and he scooped me up and strode to the bed. He rolled over me, pulling me toward him so we lay facing each other. His lips skimmed over my cheeks, kissing away the dampness left from my tears. I tugged at his shirt, drawing it up. He sat up and peeled it off, dropping it onto the floor before reaching for mine. After peeling it off he hesitated, his eyes widening slightly as he took in my bare skin and the simple white bra I wore.

And though he hadn't even touched me, I suddenly felt exposed and naïve, more naked than I'd felt when Cash had been beside me. I reached for Maximus, pulling him down on top of me. The enticing scent of my first true mate surrounded me. An instinctual need had risen within me, a need to close the gulf that had opened between us. When his bare skin touched mine, I gasped at the shock of intimacy.

Maximus drew me closer, his mouth finding mine, tasting it. His warm hands slid up my bare back, pinching the clasp of my bra to unhook it. A second later, he drew it slowly down my arm. A tremor of need shimmered through me when the cool air brushed over my bare nipple, and it hardened instantly. A soft moan escaped my throat, entering

Maximus's mouth. He groaned and ran his hand up my side, cupping my breast.

His warm hand massaged gently, his tongue sliding against mine in a slow, erotic rhythm as his thumb caressed my nipple. Heat built in my core, and I raked my nails down his back, relishing the shiver that rippled over his skin at my touch. Maximus pulled his hand back a bit, skimming the tip of my nipple with his palm until it tightened almost painfully. He pinched it between his finger and thumb, pulsing with the rhythm of his tongue. My clit throbbed, and I arched up, pressing my bare skin to his, aching for more. Drawing my knees up, I wrapped my legs around his hips, a shudder of pleasure wracking my body as his rigid length pressed between my thighs.

Being with him felt so right, so good after the distance between us all week. I dropped my head back with a sigh, letting his lips play over my chin, down my neck. Shivers raced across my skin as his mouth moved down, his lips and teeth and tongue pulling and biting gently, expertly dancing along the line between pleasure and pain. At last, I didn't think I could stand another moment. I slid my hand between us, gripping his thick cock through his pants.

"I want you inside me," I whispered.

Growling, Maximus drew away and sat up, unbuttoning my jeans and quickly tugging them down over my hips, my knees, and finally my feet. He dropped them onto the floor as if forgotten, his eyes fixed on the tangle of hair at the apex of my thighs. His lids lowered halfway, his eyes clouded with lust. Kneeling on the mattress, he lifted my feet to his shoulders.

I squirmed toward him, wanting to close the distance between us as quickly as Cash had the night before. But Maximus had other plans. He ran his hands from my ankles to my knees, then down my thighs, parting them further.

The door swung open at just that moment, and a tall, muscular black man in a pair of designer shades stepped into the room.

With a curse, Maximus threw his shirt over me, blocking my body from Jett's view.

"Don't let me stop you," Jett said with a grin, holding up both hands. "I'm a patient man. I can wait." He leaned against the wall and crossed his arms as if settling in to watch. Of course he'd chosen this moment to show up after going MIA for a week.

I pushed up on my elbows, glaring at him. "Ever heard of knocking?"

"And miss the good stuff?"

My wolf whined for more of Maximus's touch, but he'd drawn back, a scowl on his face. He got up, picked up my jeans, and handed them back.

Jett shrugged. "Looks like I missed it anyway."

"Have some decency," Maximus said, grabbing Jett's shoulder and manhandling him out of the room.

I threw myself back on the bed and pulled a pillow

over my face to muffle my groan of frustration. Maximus had gotten me all worked up for nothing, and now I was so freaking horny I could scream. Instead, I had to face all of them together and talk about politics. At least I'd smoothed things over with Maximus. Now I just had to tell the other three that I had four mates. That should be fun.

## 17

## ARIANA

I tugged my clothes back on before following Maximus and Jett out to the living room. My jaw clenched and irritation lashed through me. Though the heat burning through me had dulled some, my core still ached to be filled.

Of all the times Jett could choose to reappear, it had to be right then? I snorted and pursed my lips. Maximus shot me a questioning look, one eyebrow raised. I shook my head. It wasn't important. There'd be plenty of time for us to sneak off later.

Jett flashed a grin over his shoulder like he knew what I was thinking. Damn cat.

"What are you here for again?" I asked, my voice low with annoyance.

Jett chuckled, the sound shaking his shoulders and sending a jolt of heat directly to my center. I ground my teeth and squeezed my thighs together.

*Mine*, my wolf rumbled.

*Yeah, yeah. So you say.*

Jett leapt over the back of a plush white leather couch, sinking into the cushions and draping a relaxed arm over the back. "I have some information about your little vampire attack."

I blinked in surprise. So he wasn't here just to interrupt us.

Maximus stiffened. "What did you find out?"

I slid onto the couch's matching loveseat, and Maximus was quick to drop down beside me, sliding a possessive arm around my shoulders. I leaned back into the crook of his arm, taming my growling wolf just a little.

The smug smile on Jett's face quickly faded. "You sure you don't want to wait for the other two? Where is the Dragon Overlord anyway?" He looked around comically. "I'm surprised he'd miss spending time with Quick Silver."

"Quick Silver?" I scoffed. Was that the panther's new name for me? My wolf smiled at the pet name, while human me couldn't help crossing her arms. He was a cocky one, a fact proven by his toothy grin.

"We'll fill them in later," Maximus said, squeezing my shoulder.

Jett shrugged. "Fine by me. So, you remember how some of your little vampire friends got away during the fight, right?"

I nodded. Of course I remembered. The bloodsuckers were lucky to get away without my mates chasing them down.

"Well." Jett took a bracing breath. "One of them is human now."

"What?" Maximus barked, sitting bolt upright.

"I don't understand," I said. "Vampires can't be made human again... Can they?" I looked at Maximus for confirmation.

"Not until now," Jett said. "I wouldn't have believed it if my spies hadn't shown me proof. It matched the face of your attacker from security footage at a nearby intersection. It was a match. That vamp is now human."

"That isn't possible, Jett. Someone has their wires crossed," Maximus said.

I narrowed my eyes at Jett. This all seemed too unlikely, not to mentioned convenient that he had access to some kind of vampire spies and street footage. My chest tightened and cold pooled in my stomach. Could Jett be working with the vampires? Was this some kind of trick?

"It's real," Jett said. "Your mate has vampire curing juju in her blood." His dark gaze landed on me, inspecting me like a lab rat. There was definitely more to Jett than the bravado exterior he liked to show.

"This is crazy," I said with a shiver.

"I couldn't agree more," Jett said. "But stranger things have happened." His gaze slid from me to

Maximus, and I could have sworn jealousy flashed in his eyes.

My wolf rumbled for freedom, and I quickly clamped down on her overzealous urges. Jett might be one of my mates, but if he was a traitor to shifterkind, I didn't want him in our lives. Even if my wolf cried at the thought of losing him.

The elevator dinged then, and the three of us turned just in time to see Cash and Owen walking in. Cash flashed a smirk and gave me a wink the moment his eyes landed on me. My blood heated in response. Owen brushed his hair back and gave me a lopsided smile.

"Welcome to the party!" Jett opened his arms and grinned, his bravado returning.

Cash raised an eyebrow. "Did I miss something?"

"Ariana's blood turned a vamp human," Maximus said.

Cash's eyes widened, and Owen's mouth dropped open.

"Explain," Cash snapped.

Jett seemed delighted by their reactions. "Like wolf-boy said, my spies informed me of it a few hours ago. One of the vamps that bit Quick Silver and got away is human now."

"That's impossible," Owen said.

"That's what I'm saying," I grumbled.

Owen took a seat on the couch a good two feet

away from Jett while Cash began pacing the living room.

Jett shrugged like he didn't care if they thought he was lying. He'd done his duty in bringing the information forward. I pursed my lips. I could feel slivers of Maximus's trust through the bond. Even if the clans had been at war for years, the alphas did seem to trust what Jett was saying.

But I couldn't shake my suspicions completely.

"What does this mean?" Cash said. He stopped and turned to face us.

"That life's about to get a whole lot more dangerous for Ariana." Maximus drew me closer to his side.

I barely resisted the urge to snuggle against him. Overwhelming myself with his mouthwatering scent wasn't going to help me think clearly. "We can handle it."

"Of course we can," Cash said. He looked at me pointedly.

I bit my tongue on a groan. Why did I have a feeling they were about to chain me in a tower like Rapunzel?

"As long as we stick together, everything will be fine," Owen said, my voice of reason. He gave me a sweet smile, and I relaxed. I wanted to go curl up in his arms suddenly, but after what had happened earlier, I didn't think leaving Maximus's side to go sit in the lap of another was a great idea. Especially with the whole *four mates* thing still hanging in the air.

"Exactly," I said. "We can continue visiting the other clans. We'll just have to be more vigilant."

Maximus stiffened. "I don't think that's a good idea."

Of course he didn't.

"I'm not going to stay locked up at the pack's lodge." I turned from Maximus to Cash. "Or this apartment. So you're all going to have to live with it."

Maximus's body vibrated with his growl, but he didn't argue.

"Well, I'll let you kids sort it out." Jett stood and stretched, his tight black shirt rising to reveal a deep V descending into his low-slung jeans.

My eyes widened and my blood pumped, filling me with heat. My wolf howled *mine* and clawed for the surface.

*Down girl.* I gulped and forced my gaze away, but not before Jett caught me looking. His cocky grin returned, and he dropped his shades over his eyes before rounding the couch to head for the door.

"Let us know if you find out anything else," Cash said.

"Will do." Jett gave a mock salute before he disappeared down the hall to the elevator.

"I don't think continuing the tour of the clans is a good idea," Maximus said as soon as the elevator doors dinged shut.

"It'll be fine," I said.

"It will," Owen added. "We're head to bear territory next. She'll be safe with my clan."

I shot him a grateful smile.

"I suppose we can't get out of it," Maximus said. "I'll allow it to continue as long as you don't go anywhere without one of us."

I looked around at the three gorgeous men with me. My mates. I could hardly believe I was so lucky.

"Deal," I said.

Cash twisted his jaw. "We don't take any risks…"

"Not with Ariana. Ever," Maximus said.

Owen nodded.

My mates had finally come to an agreement. Protecting me seemed to be the only goal they had in common. I could only hope I wouldn't need it, and they were all worrying for nothing.

## 18

## ARIANA

Ignoring my wolf, who was growling on about not having laid claim to Jett, I turned to Cash. "Do you have access to the garage from up here?"

"What do you mean?" he asked.

"Could you lock the door?" I asked. "I need to talk to Jett before he disappears again."

"What for?" Maximus asked, eyeing me suspiciously.

"Actually, I need to talk to all of you," I said. I might as well get it all out in the open. If they were my mates, they might be affected by this weird vampire-curing blood of mine. Not in the way vampires were affected, of course, but in a more someone-might-want-to-murder-them way. I'd told Maximus that I had four mates already, but the others deserved to know, too.

Cash was lounging on the sofa, dropping winks in my direction every time Maximus looked away, silently gloating at the knowledge that he'd fucked Maximus's mate. The alphas might respect each other politically, but that didn't mean they were above battling for dominance in other areas. Frankly, his cockiness was making me regret the night before.

I might actually enjoy seeing his face when I told him he had to share me with three other men.

"Jett's not going to be happy when he finds out he can't get out of the garage," Maximus said as Cash tapped on the screen of his phone.

"He can get out," Cash said with a smug smile. "He just can't get his car out."

A few minutes later, Jett came storming back into the room. "What the fuck," he shouted at Cash. "You're holding me hostage now? What is this shit?"

Cash shot to his feet, a growl in his throat at being challenged. "Don't forget, you're in my house."

"I'm well aware," Jett said. "Seeing as I can't get out of it."

"No one's holding you hostage," Owen said quietly. "Ariana wants to talk to us before you go."

Jett turned his furious eyes on me. "You couldn't talk to me five minutes ago when I was up here?"

"The Silver Shifter would like a word with the alphas of the four clans," Maximus said. "It's within her rights to ask for an audience with us."

"You didn't stick around long enough to give me a

chance," I said to Jett. I wasn't going to let him talk to me that way, and I sure as hell wasn't going to let Maximus answer for me. I appreciated his standing up for me, though, especially since I knew how painful my announcement was for him. I sent him a rush of love through our bond before sitting up straight and shrugging his arm from my shoulders. If I was so damn important, I could have my own voice.

"If you don't want to be included in conversations that affect your clan, that's your choice. I thought I'd show you the courtesy of offering before we made decisions without your input. We've all been here discussing the welfare of the clans for weeks, and you haven't participated. I thought you might have showed up to rectify that, not just to deliver your news, turn around, and pull a disappearing act again."

Jett crossed his impressive arms and stared down at me with hooded eyes. "Looked like you were real busy discussing the future of the clans when I got here," he said. "But hey, if that's how we do business now, we can take this to the bedroom. Would it help if my head was between your thighs for this conversation?"

"It might help if you took your head out of your ass," I shot back, my face hot.

Maximus snarled at Jett, but Jett ignored him. His hostile gaze was locked on mine. I wasn't about to back down. My wolf growled inside me, and I bared my teeth at Jett.

Cash took a step toward him, looming over Jett as if trying to intimidate him. Jett didn't seem to notice. His dark eyes narrowed, his nostrils flaring as we stared each other down.

My wolf growled louder, no longer wanting to mate. She sensed danger, and she wanted out. She wanted to fight.

"I get the feeling I'm missing something," Owen said, shifting uncomfortably. His gaze moved between the rest of us, looking utterly lost.

"Ariana," Maximus said. "Care to explain to them what's going on?"

"Yes," Jett said, pursing his gorgeous lips. "Do explain."

"All right, guys, let's all have a seat and calm down," Owen said. "There's a lot of tension in here right now."

"I'll relax when I know this isn't an ambush," Jett said, his glare turning back to Cash.

"I'm unlocking the garage right now," Cash said, pulling out his phone and tapping something on the screen. He showed it to Jett, who gave a grunt and took a seat on the couch, apparently satisfied.

"Spit it out, Quick Silver," Jett said with a scowl. "I've got more important things to do than lounge around a dragon's lair making eyes at everyone."

I gritted my teeth in annoyance, then turned to face the the others. Maximus's protectiveness made me feel safe to speak. Owen's quiet strength gave me courage. Cash's certainty steadied me. And Jett, well, he pissed me off just enough for me to enjoy breaking this news.

"I admit, until Maximus pulled me out of the pits, I'd never even heard of the Silver Shifter," I said. "I'm not sure of all my duties and responsibilities. Maximus tells me I'm also supposed to have some special skill."

"The last Silver Shifter was an oracle," Cash said.

"Have you discovered your power already?" Owen asked, clasping his huge paws between his knees and leaning forward.

"No," I said. "But I do know one thing."

My heart suddenly thudded hard in my chest, and nerves overtook me. What if they were all as pissed as Maximus had been? What if they hurt each other?

My wolf was having none of that. She snarled at the very thought of anyone—even one of them—hurting her mates.

Cash gave a cocky grin. "Tell them, Ari."

Maximus put a hand on my thigh and gave it an encouraging squeeze while glaring daggers at Cash.

"I've already told three of you separately," I said. "But I wanted everyone to know. My wolf has claimed all of you."

Jett snorted loudly.

"Well, she hasn't officially claimed you, Jett," I said, my face warming at the realization that he now knew exactly what was going on inside my head. At least the primal, wolf part of my brain.

"Wait a second..." Cash said.

"I know," I said. "When we were together, our animals claimed each other. But my wolf had already claimed Maximus. And Owen."

"She didn't claim me," Jett said.

"So, you're not my mate," Cash said. "You're still Maximus's."

"I'm both," I said. "You felt the bond. You know I'm your mate."

"Yeah," Cash said. "I know I am. But I didn't know they were."

"I've already shared that bond with Maximus," I said. "And it's still there. My wolf claimed him as her mate, as she should. And then she claimed Owen."

"And then me," Cash said.

"Each of you means something different to me," I said. "But I can't choose between you. You are all equally important, and my wolf claims you equally as her mates."

"How's this going to work, Ari?" Cash asked. "You can't have more than one mate."

"She does, though," Maximus said quietly. I could feel the hurt lingering in our bond when he said the words, and I took his hand, linking my fingers with his. He might not have been my first, but he'd been my rescuer, the person who brought me back to life. Our bond was deeper than physical.

"It's one way to unite the clans," Owen said slowly. "You have to admit it hasn't been done before."

"For good reason," Jett said.

"And the clans are always at odds," Owen said. "With one mate to unite all our alphas…"

"Unite the clans?" Jett asked incredulously. "Sharing one mate sounds like a good way to start an all-out war. Shit, don't you white people love the story of Helen of Troy?"

"I'm not trying to turn anyone against each other," I said. "I'm only telling you what's happened. Obviously I'm not going to force you to be my mate."

"Then remind me why I'm here," Jett said.

"I just thought you should know," I said. "My wolf thinks you're her mate, too, Jett. Trust me when I say I'm no more crazy about the idea than you are."

"Now I know," he said, standing. "If the garage is open and I'm free to go, I'll just be going."

"Can you honestly say your panther isn't telling you the same thing?" I asked. I knew his panther was in agreement. He had to be.

Didn't he?

"It doesn't matter what he's saying," Jett said. "I don't make important decisions with my dick or my panther. Not all men are animals, Quick Silver."

"Yeah, but all the men in this room are," I pointed out.

Cash laughed, Owen shrugged in agreement, and Maximus gave a low growl beside me.

"I'm out," Jett said with another mock salute. "I'll see you when you reach my clan."

I couldn't help but wonder if he'd ever accept me as his mate, and if he didn't, what kinds of problems that might cause.

## 19

## ARIANA

I tilted my head back and groaned as the savory taste of hollandaise sauce filled my mouth. Oh, the things I'd been missing out on while in the pits. Not only had I missed out on four utterly gorgeous mates for the last decade or so, I'd also missed out on fast cars, sex, and eggs benedict.

Ask me yesterday, and I would have said the thing I'd most missed out on was my sexy mates. Today? I wasn't so sure.

"Enjoying yourself?" Cash chuckled as he walked into the kitchen.

I looked up from my plate and gulped down the lump of eggs I'd been salivating over. "Yes."

He took a seat on the stool next to me. The chef flashed a quick grin and nodded a greeting before he returned to making his boss a serving of his own.

"You're leaving on the rest of your tour today, right?" Cash asked.

"You're not coming?" I asked before taking another bite. This time I restrained my moan—just barely.

Cash sighed. "I wish I could. Urgent Dragon Council business calls."

I took a sip of freshly squeezed orange juice before answering. "That's unfortunate."

A loud yawn broke through the constant sizzling on the stove, and we turned to find Owen slipping into the kitchen with a red plaid shirt hanging loose over a tight grey t-shirt. He stretched and ran a hand through his hair. I couldn't help but eye the tautness of his shirt over his sculpted pecs. Now I was licking my lips for a whole other reason.

"Good morning," he said, flashing me a lopsided grin before he took the stool on my other side. "Maximus isn't up yet?"

"He said he had a few calls to make." I gestured toward the living room, the direction in which Maximus had taken off.

Owen nodded in understanding before twining his hand in the hair at the base of my neck and pulling me toward him. He kissed the top of my head before releasing me. My heart fluttered and warmth coiled in my belly.

"Time to go." Maximus appeared in the doorway, his cellphone still in hand and a troubled look on his face.

"What's going on?" I asked. Unease filled our bond, and my appetite waned.

"Jett sent another update about the vampire situation. Something is brewing, but he isn't sure what."

The warmth in my stomach cooled. My hand went to my neck, and I tried to suppress a shiver as I recalled the feeling of being bitten by the bloodsuckers.

Owen laid a large hand on the small of my back, comforting me somewhat. "As long as we take the backroads like we planned, we should be fine."

Maximus nodded. "Yeah. We don't want any vamps catching your scent, Ariana."

My fingers tightened around the hem of my sweater. Apparently, Cash had some women's clothes just lying around, perfectly my size. Apparently, he had a type.

"I've got to take off now too," Cash said. "I'll meet up with you tonight."

I reached out and squeezed his hand as he slid off the stool beside me. "Be careful."

Cash smiled and leaned in for a quick kiss. Though it lasted only a second, it warmed me to my core.

"Ready?" Maximus asked, shifting uncomfortably. He'd verbally agreed to my need for four mates, but I could tell he hadn't fully accepted the truth of it yet. He definitely hadn't liked seeing Cash kiss me—or feeling my reaction to it. Still, he hadn't tried to stop us, or ripped Cash's head off, so we were making progress. If I wanted to keep peace not just between clans but in my own life, I'd have to be more sensitive to my mates' feelings about sharing until we were all settled into our relationship.

For now, though, I had less personal concerns to occupy my thoughts. I took a deep breath and forced an easy smile. "Yeah. Let's head out."

"There aren't any vampire hangouts on the way to bear territory," Owen said. "We should be safe."

That made me feel better. Maybe we'd get lucky and escape to bear territory unharmed.

THE CAR RUMBLED beneath me as we pulled through the back streets headed toward the bridge out of town. So Maximus wasn't the only one with a clan outside the city. If that was true, then I wondered why Cash chose to stay in the city. Wait. That was easy. Cash loved fast cars and shiny things. Of course he liked the city.

"When was the last time you were in bear territory?" Owen asked Maximus from the back seat. Today, we rode together in a black sedan with tinted windows. It was the most inconspicuous car Cash owned and the least likely to be picked out by the vampires. Or so we hoped.

"It's been awhile," Maximus said. He glanced at Owen in the rearview mirror. "Maybe a decade ago?"

My eyebrows furrowed. "So you were like fifteen?"

Again, Maximus and Owen exchanged a look in the mirror. "Not exactly," Maximus said.

"How old were you?" I asked. Come to think of it, how exactly did most shifters age? I seemed to age as fast as anyone else, but Maximus didn't look much older than me. From what I'd heard from Cash, dragons lived for a long time. The Silver Shifter showed up every hundred years and married the alpha of that clan. So the Silver Dragon had married the dragon alpha, who was Cash's dad, almost a hundred years ago. I wasn't sure how I felt about a ninety-year-old guy taking my virginity, but it was a little late to think of that now.

Maximus chuckled. "A little older than fifteen."

I crossed my arms. Well, that was a disappointing answer.

"He's just being shy," Owen teased from the back seat.

"He's something all right," I said.

The squeal of tires pulled my attention back to the street.

"Ariana!" Maximus shouted. His arm slammed against my chest, pushing me into the seat.

A crash jolted through the entire car, sending us flying. A tiny scream escaped me, and I tried to cling to my seat as the sound of tearing metal screeched through the interior.

Ringing filled my ears from the terrible sound, and I fought the urge to clamp my hands over them. A black SUV pulled up outside as the one that hit us slammed on the gas. The smell of burned rubber flew up my nose as the SUV pushed us across the street. I ground my teeth as the noise only got louder, and then my heart leapt into my throat. The car beneath us shifted, and my entire world flew in a loop as we rolled off the road and into the ditch.

I braced my palms against the dashboard, a scream caught in my throat. The windshield shattered, and shards cut my cheeks. I inhaled sharply and squeezed my eyes closed. Bits of plastic, metal and glass battered my body and my seatbelt dug into my torso so hard I was sure it'd bruise.

The pressure of Maximus's arm disappeared, and my stomach bottomed out like I was riding in Cash's Ferrari again. My breath was torn from my lungs, and I held onto my seatbelt as another crash and screech filled my ears. Pain tore through my skull as something hard collided with it. A wave of dizziness and nausea hit me, and then blackness swallowed me.

## 20

## ARIANA

Wind buffeted my ears, and silver hair whipped my face and shoulders as I came to. I blinked slowly, clawing my way from the darkness behind my eyelids. My eyebrows furrowed as I registered cold, hard concrete beneath me. Why was I lying on the ground? Had I been thrown from the car? That couldn't be right. I'd been wearing a seatbelt.

Confusion filled me as I opened my eyes. My hair filled most of my vision, but beyond that I could see the slab of concrete I was lying on, and then the rooftops of skyscrapers.

What the hell was going on?

I tried to move, but everything hurt. I groaned and squeezed my eyes shut as pain shot up my knees. I must have hit them on the dash of the car when we crashed. Or when someone crashed into *us*.

My breath caught. Wait. Maximus and Owen were with me in that car.

I opened my eyes to find a dark clouded sky. My breaths turned into pants as my heart raced. My mates. Where were they?

Despite the pain, I twisted onto my stomach so I could push up onto my knees and stand. Before I could, I froze. A few feet away, six men and women with deathly pale skin stood facing my mate.

Maximus groaned as he curled on the ground. Thick chains shackled his wrists and ankles. Considering he hadn't torn free, I knew they had to be silver. One of the vampires held a long silver dagger, blood dripping from its tip.

*No.* No, no, no. If they'd cut him with silver, it would poison him. He needed help now!

Pain tore through our bond and then panic as Maximus realized I was awake.

"Maximus," I said. I pushed myself onto my knees, cursing my shifter healing for not working fast enough. "*Maximus.*"

One of the female vampires pulled back and delivered a swift kick to Maximus's spine. Anger rolled through me, burning a path straight to my wolf. She snarled to life, pushing at my skin for release.

"Oh, the little Silver Shifter is awake," a male voice said.

I turned to see a man with shoulder-length black hair smirking at me. His eyes flashed red, and twin fangs poked his bottom lip. He'd fit the definition of classically handsome—straight out of a Victorian romance novel. But the bloodthirsty look in his eyes sent a shiver down my spine.

"Who the hell are you?" I growled. I clenched my fists and forced myself to my feet. Heavy winds buffeted my sides, and I stumbled, barely able to get my feet under me before I crashed to the ground again.

"Viktor Bancroft." The vampire gave me a mocking bow. His grin spread so wide when he straightened that he displayed his teeth. "A pleasure to meet you, Silver Shifter."

The other vampires had stepped away, snarling and hissing at me like I was poison.

To them, I was.

"Wish I could say the same," I said. My hands fisted at my sides. I could barely feel Maximus. His consciousness flickered in and out from the beating they'd delivered, and worse, the silver tainting his blood. If these vampires thought they were getting out of this alive, they were damn wrong. Not only had they kidnapped us, but they'd hurt my mate, and that was unforgivable.

Viktor chuckled. "You're a feisty one. No wonder the alphas like you."

My gaze snapped back to the vampire. What did he know about the alphas? Had Jett been coluding with them the whole time?

"I see you're confused," Viktor continued. "Don't worry, you won't be for much longer." He held his hands behind his back and circled me like a wolf stalking its prey.

I suddenly felt like I was back in the pits with the vampire gatekeepers rattling our cages and sticking silver clubs inside to provoke us. I took a deep breath. I wasn't going to take the bait.

He frowned when I didn't. "Don't you want to know why you're here?"

"I'm the cure for vampirism. Why else would I be here?"

His sadistic grin returned. "Smart girl. I like that."

I turned to face him. I didn't want to take my eyes off him even as he circled me. "So, you're what? The big bad villain at the end of the Disney movie?" I tried to distract him while my mind raced to come up with a way out of this.

Six vampires. Two of us.

My heart skipped a beat. *Owen*. Where was he? He'd been in the car with us. I took a quick look around the roof, but he was nowhere to be found.

"Something like that," Viktor said. "Maybe the boss of the big bad."

"Uh huh. So you're the Evil Queen, and these are your huntsmen?" I took a steadying breath. *Calm down, Ari. We need to find a way out of this.*

Viktor tilted his head back and laughed. "Oh my, you are a treat. It's too bad you're a filthy mutt with venom in your veins. I'd love to have a taste of you. The vampire you turned said your blood was just divine." He eyed my neck. I had to actively resist covering it with my hands.

"Too bad," I said. There was a rooftop exit about fifteen feet away. If Maximus could stay awake long enough to distract at least two, I might be able to get the upper hand on Viktor here and surprise them all into a quick death by my wolf's teeth before getting rid of the ones guarding Maximus. They couldn't bite me if they wanted to stay vampires. All they could do was toss me around a little.

"Forgive me, I'm wasting your last moments." Viktor smirked. "I'm sorry to say that you cannot exist, not while vampires walk the earth. You endanger us all with your blood, so we need to eradicate you."

"I don't suppose you'd reconsider?" I kept talking while trying to catch Maximus's attention. He was up on all fours now, but from the way he was holding his stomach, he had to be severely injured. I could feel it. When I paused to sink into the bond, I could feel Maximus's pain as if it were my own. Every breath was agony, tearing through his chest. They must have stabbed his stomach or lung.

Shit. He wasn't going to be able to help me like that.

Viktor chuckled. "Wish I could, dearie. But the Lamia Queen has sentenced you to death."

"The who?"

"So naive. So ignorant." Viktor stepped closer, and I instinctively stepped back. He smiled as I did. Each step drove me further from Maximus and closer to the edge of the roof.

I was literally backing myself into a corner. I had to stop. The next time Viktor stepped forward, I steeled myself and remained motionless. His smile turned into a frown. He stepped forward again, and again, but I didn't let him back me any closer to the edge.

"Say goodbye to your precious pet, alpha," Viktor said over his shoulder.

Maximus looked up, his eyes flashing yellow and pain twisting his expression. He lurched from his knees up onto one foot. "A-Ariana."

My heart raced. "Maximus. It's okay. I'm going to get us out of this."

Viktor closed the distance between us, his hand wrapping around my throat. I gasped and pulled back, but his fingers clamped tighter until I fought to breathe. "No, you aren't, Silver Shifter."

I tore at his fingers as he continued to put pressure on my neck. He lifted me, and I clawed at his fingers. My wolf howled for freedom. I took one last breath, ready to let her take over.

Viktor threw me. I sailed through the air, wind pounding against my eardrums. I twisted to get my hands under me before I crashed into the building. But as I turned, the lip of the roof appeared, and I sailed right passed it.

What had to be nearly a hundred stories below lay the streets of New York City.

My heart stopped as I looked death in the face. Only it wasn't an opponent like I'd always thought. It wasn't another shifter in the pits or a vampire tearing out my throat—it was a fall that no one could survive.

As I plummeted toward the ground, fear shot through my every limb like a geyser.

Maximus's panic and anguish joined mine, and I thought of all the things we'd miss out on. I'd never really know my mates or what life could be like when I was free. I'd only been free from my endless torment for a few weeks, and it was all about to be stolen away from me.

Fury replaced my fear, and heat burned through my veins. It wasn't fair. My whole life had been survival. Fight to survive. Fight to eat. Fight because there was nothing left. And now I didn't need to fight anymore. Or so I had hoped.

My fingers tightened into fists as the ground came up at me all too fast. I squeezed my eyes shut and pictured my mates. Maximus. Owen. Cash. Even Jett.

As the image of the dragon shifter sailed through my mind, my blood began to burn. Fire tore through my entire being, heating me from the inside out. I opened my eyes only to see red. A scream tore from my throat, and then I felt it. The change. But instead of a wolf tearing from my skin, it was something else. My wolf wasn't a wolf anymore, but a beast.

The beast writhed inside of me and clawed at my control, demanding I free her. With the fiery pain enveloping me, I let the beast out.

For a second, there was only blackness. I thought I'd finally hit the ground, and this was death. There was no afterlife—when you died you were just gone. But the next instant my eyes opened and the windows of the skyscraper were still sailing past.

Rage was all I felt as my wings pushed me up into the sky.

Wait. *Wings*?

The beast took over, pulling me through the air until we flew over the lip of the roof. There, lying on the concrete was our mate. Blood poured from the corner of Maximus's mouth and his abdomen, pooling around him. One of the vampires grabbed his arm and dragged him up. That was all it took for my beast to crash down on the edge of the building.

A roar tore from my throat, vibrating through my very soul. How *dare* they harm my mate? How *dare* they try to kill me and what was mine?

The vampires turned to face me, eyes wide and mouths agape. Good. Let them be afraid. Let my beast be the last thing they saw before I tore them to pieces.

My chest rumbled with a growl, and heat burned in my throat. I pushed back onto my hind legs, flapping my enormous silver wings. The vampires lifted their arms to block the wind, but there was no blocking my fire.

Heat poured from my mouth, and fire tore across the roof of the building. The closest of the vampires was caught in the blast. As fire consumed her, she screamed before turning to ash.

The vampires reared back, but one more was caught in the death my flames provided. A male leapt at me with the speed only a vampire could conjure. I snarled and whipped in a circle. My tail thrashed into his side. I heard the cracks of a hundred bones, and then his body was sailing through the air, over the skyscrapers of New York.

I spun back around as a bite of pain snapped through my front leg. Flames poured from my mouth, over my scales, and dusted the bloodsucker.

The last two sprinted for the roof's stairwell. I descended onto all fours, rushing forward. I sailed over my injured mate and snapped Viktor between my jaws. Fresh rage poured through me, and I roared as I threw him into the air. He screamed as he plummeted back toward the roof—and right down my throat.

Smoke blew from my nostrils as I swung to face the last vampire. He raced away from the stairwell toward the edge of the roof, but I caught him in my powerful jaws, slamming my teeth shut until blood gushed into my maw. He howled in pain, and I squeezed tighter until the sounds stopped. I tossed the body to the side. It tasted disgusting, like death and ash on my tongue.

My body heaved with heat as I turned, making

sure there were no more enemies for me to defeat. A growl rumbled in my throat as I prowled the rooftop.

"Ariana?" Maximus struggled to sit, his eyes wide with fear and hope.

I swung to face him, blinking slowly. Ariana. Right.

As I looked down at myself, I wasn't human or wolf. And I wasn't just a beast like my mind would have me believe. I sorted through my thoughts, trying to pry myself free until I realized what the scales and wings and fire meant.

I was a dragon.

The realization slammed into me with such force I almost backed off the edge of the building. My heart raced, and my mind pulled in all different directions. This wasn't possible. But it was happening. I was in the body of a dragon. No. I *was* the dragon.

A whimper escaped me in a deep rumble. What was going on? This couldn't be real.

Pain burned through me suddenly, and I realized what it was. My beast was so tired she wanted to transform back to my human state. But I couldn't let her, not yet. I had to get us out of there first.

I turned back to my mate as I assured my beast she only had to hold on for a few more minutes.

Maximus reached out a hand to touch me. I dipped my large head to press the tip of my long snout to his hand.

"Ariana," he sighed. I felt his intense relief through our bond. "You're alive."

I nodded and nudged him with my nose. I wasn't sure how much longer he'd be alive, though. If I didn't get help soon, he might not make it. Pain rippled through me again. *Just a few minutes*, I told my dragon.

I reared up onto my hind legs, flapping my great wings, and lifted off the top of the building. Maximus looked at me in confusion before I dove back down and grabbed him in one of my clawed hands.

His arms wrapped weakly around one of my legs, and he held on as I sailed through the sky. It took nearly five minutes to fly out of the city back toward pack territory. Every minute was like agony tearing through every fiber of my body. My beast was growing weaker and weaker, drifting further away from me.

The lodge came into view through the trees, and I huffed a relieved sigh. But I'd never landed before. Even though flying seemed to come easily, my beast had been in control for that. But as she drifted to the back of my mind, panic stole me, and pain forced its way directly into my head.

I cried out as I plummeted toward the ground. I could feel Maximus's distress, but I could hardly pay attention to it with the ringing filling my head. Heat began to burn across my skin. I was changing in midair.

I hit the ground while half shifted, my entire body on fire and my head feeling like razors shook within my skull. I gripped my hair as the pain began to subside, and I became fully human.

## 21

## OWEN

I woke up to the pain of a sledgehammer pounding inside my skull. Grabbing my head, I sat up, my eyes searching out my mate. The doors of the car stood open, and her side of the seat was empty. Shards of glass glittered across every surface in the car, but Ariana was nowhere to be found. Maximus was also missing, but I found myself far less concerned with his welfare than hers.

I yanked at the handle of my door only to find it immovable, the metal crushed inward. I started for the open door, but a stab of pain in my leg stopped me short. My legs were trapped. *Damn it.*

My bear was fighting to get out, to charge down the streets roaring for my mate. The vamps had gotten her. I might have hit my head, but I remembered that all too well. They'd run us off the road and taken the other two, presumably leaving me for dead. Or maybe they just didn't want the hassle of pulling me out of the car. My legs felt as if they'd been cemented in place.

I practiced a minute of meditation, trying to clear my mind enough to figure out what to do next. When I opened my eyes, I knew. I had to find Ari.

Bracing my hands against the crushed metal, I heaved with all my strength. With a squeal of protest, the frame of the car bent a bit. I threw my weight against it again, pounding at it until I'd freed my legs. Only my bear strength allowed me to free myself without calling in the Jaws of Life. I dragged myself across the seat and stood on aching, injured legs. I scented the air but caught no sign of Ari's jasmine scent on the breeze.

Pulling my phone from my pocket, I dialed Jett and then added Cash into the conference call.

"I know you're busy with the Dragon Council today, but it's going to have to wait," I said. "Ari's been taken by the vamps."

"What?" Cash barked into the phone.

Jett swore quietly. I imagined if I were him, I'd be pretty torn up that I had left things so unresolved and hostile between my mate and I.

"They ran us off the road and took Ari and Maximus," I said. "We need to find them now."

"How?" Cash asked.

"I'll have everyone going over the camera feeds from the last hour," Jett said. Tapping in the background alerted me to Jett typing frantically. "Let's see if I have any footage of an abduction. I'll contact my moles and see if word has reached them yet."

"And what are we supposed to do?" Cash snarled. "Sit on our asses and wait while Ari's in danger?"

"I'll alert the bears," I said. "I'm closer to Maximus's home than my own, so I'll stop and alert them, too."

"They'll know if Maximus is in danger," Jett said. "Through the pack bond."

Damn werewolves had it so good. I only wished I could communicate with my clan as easily.

"Then maybe they'll know more than we do," I said. "Besides, if they get free, they're most likely to go home."

The words left a hollow feeling in my belly. I didn't like to think of Ariana's home being with just Maximus. I had wanted to show her my home, to share my family with her. Instead of being safe and secure in bear territory, she was probably being tortured—or worse—by those sick bloodsuckers.

"We'll meet you there," Cash said before hanging up.

"I'll come get you," Jett said quietly.

"I'm on my way now," I said, loping off down the street, leaving the crumpled car behind.

"I know," Jett said. "I have you on one of my surveillance cameras now. I'll be there in ten."

I was glad for the ride when Jett arrived, as it

would get me there faster than even my bear form could take me. And it wasn't like I could run to Maximus's pack land in bear form. I would have done it if I could. Sitting in the car doing nothing while Ariana was in danger nearly drove me mad. Everything in me longed to get out, to run to her, to fight my way to her. But I had no idea where they'd taken her.

The moment we pulled up at Maximus's lodge, a dozen wolves were on the vehicle, yanking the doors open and dragging us out.

"We're here as allies," I said quickly, holding up my hands in surrender to the woman baring her teeth at me—Maximus's second, I remembered.

I quickly filled them in on everything I knew. A minute later, Cash's car skidded to a stop in a spray of gravel, and he leapt out to join us.

"Any word?" he asked.

"Maximus is gravely injured," said Shira, the second-in-command.

"What about Ari?" I demanded.

Jett's phone chimed and he checked the screen. "We've got her," he said, holding up the screen where a grainy video played.

"Then let's go," I said, turning back to his car.

"This was taken almost an hour ago," Jett said. "But we can use it to track where they took her."

"No need," Shira said. Her eyes lit up, though her gaze looked far away. I realized she was focusing on the bond. "They've gotten free."

It was all I could do not to grab the woman and shake her. "How is Ari?" I asked, measuring my words. I tried to channel some inner peace, but there was no peace inside me when it came to someone hurting my mate.

"She's..."

"She's there," Cash cried, leaping toward the trees. I looked for her to come staggering out of the forest, though I had no idea how she could have gotten here so fast. It wasn't until a shadow fell across the grass that I looked up.

A silver dragon came blasting through the treetops in a shower of leaves. A body hung from its talons, and it seemed unable to carry it any longer. It careened into the yard, growing smaller by the second. Then its eyes closed, and it's enormous body slammed into the ground, upending earth with the force of its landing.

"It's Ari!" Cash said, running forward.

I would have thought he was crazy if I hadn't seen it with my own eyes. It *was* Ari. She was already partially shifted, and there was no mistaking that silver hair, the same color as her dragon scales.

"Ari," I cried, running to her and dropping to my knees. "Come back to us, baby. You're going to be okay." I didn't know what I was saying, what promises I was making. Just that she had to be okay. I'd barely gotten a moment with my mate. I couldn't lose her yet.

She finished shifting, and her body looked so small and frail compared to the creature she had been when she blasted the top off half the trees on that side of the yard. Leaves and twigs and small branches littered the grass around us.

"I'm okay," she said, her eyes opening but not quite focusing on me. "Max... Silver poison... Vampires beat him..."

"We'll take care of Maximus," Shira said. "We should get them inside. These vampires are getting awfully bold to attack our alpha."

A beat of silence followed her words. I hadn't thought beyond getting Ariana back. I hadn't considered the ramifications of the attack. Vampires had attacked the alphas of two clans in broad daylight, obviously meaning to kill us both. And not just our mate, but the Silver Shifter. This could mean war, not between the clans, but between the shifters and vampires. The conflict between clans seemed like a petty squabble in comparison to all-out war with the entire vampire nation. If the shifters didn't present a united front against the vampires, we had no chance whatsoever.

I looked down at our only chance lying in the dirt, semi-conscious. We needed her if we were to win this war with the vampires. We needed her if we were to unite the clans. But more than that, I needed her as Ariana, my mate, my only chance at more than winning. My only chance at happiness.

"I'm going to take you inside," I said, leaning down to gather Ariana into my arms with all the tenderness and care I possessed. "We'll worry about the vampires later. Right now, we're only worried about you."

The werewolves had lifted Maximus, and I followed them into Maximus's lodge with Ariana in my arms. Cash and Jett hurried behind. At the top of the stairs, I hesitated. I could take Ariana to the room in which we'd shared an intimate moment—her room. But something told me she belonged in the master bedroom now. I strode along the hall and into Maximus's room, where several wolves had gathered.

"He's going to be fine," Shira said. "His healing abilities were suppressed by the silver, but now that he's taken the antidote, he's healing already."

"And Ari?" Cash asked.

I wouldn't have wanted to be on the receiving end of the look she gave him. "I'd think you could answer that question better than I could," she snapped. "Her wounds are those of a dragon, yes?"

In typical werewolf fashion, she didn't attempt to hide her slight feeling of superiority over other shifters. Cash didn't seem to take offense. As I lay Ariana on the bed next to Maximus, Cash leaned over her and smoothed her hair from her forehead. "I can't tell without talking to her," he said. "But she might have simply overdone it."

"She's burning up," Maximus muttered.

"Good, you're awake," Shira said.

"Can we have the room?" I asked.

Shira gave me a knowing look, the same one she'd

leveled at me after I'd shared intimate moments with Ariana. Now, I knew I had nothing to feel guilty for. We were all Ariana's mates, and I had the same claim to her that Maximus did. And she had the same claim to me.

We were all in this now, bound together by the Silver Shifter in a way I could never have predicted or imagined. And yet, as the wolves left us alone in the room with her, I felt the completeness of our group. Even Jett stayed, though he stood back, a troubled frown on his face, as the rest of gathered on Maximus's huge bed waiting for our mate to awaken. Though she wasn't an oracle, our Silver Shifter held our future in her hands.

*To be continued...*

~

Follow Ari and her mates in the next installment, coming April 9th.

## A NOTE FROM THE AUTHORS

Whether you enjoyed *Silver Shifter: Her Wolf* or not, please consider leaving a review on Amazon, and/or Goodreads! Every review helps get the book in the hands of new readers, and is extremely helpful!

Thank you so much for reading, and we hope to see you again in the next book!

# SILVER SHIFTER

## 2

### HER DRAGON

# PREVIEW

## CHAPTER ONE

ARIANA

I woke slowly with a warm glow filling my whole body, though I was so exhausted I didn't think I could move even a single muscle. Not even my eyelids. A sense of contentment had settled in my belly and radiated outwards. I didn't want to move, but my curiosity took over and lifted my lids for me. I found myself lying on my back in a strange bed.

What the hell? The last thing I remembered, I'd been riding in Owen's car on the way to bear territory. And then...

Shit. Vampires had attacked.

Before I could freak out, my wolf clued me in on my surroundings. She was happy. I wasn't in a silver cage surrounded by vampires. I was safe and surrounded by my mates. Max lay on one side of me, his hand resting protectively on my waist. His eyes were closed and his dark hair fell across his forehead.

Owen lay on my other side, his big hand gently enfolding mine. His blue eyes were fixed on me and his long blond hair spilled across the pillow beside him. Cash paced beside the bed while Jett leaned against the wall, frowning at his phone as he tapped at the screen frantically. Apparently, whatever had happened was worthy of his presence but not his attention.

I opened my mouth to speak, but my throat felt like it had been incinerated by a blow torch. Grinding my teeth against the pain, I forced the words out. "What happened?"

Cash jumped about two feet in the air, which would have been funny if not for the pulsing pain in my throat. "Get her some water," he said, rushing to the bed.

Water. Fuck yes. I felt like I could drink a five-gallon bucket of ice water and it still wouldn't quench my thirst.

Owen and Max both reached for the glass of water on the bedside table. They both snatched it up at once, then paused to glare at each other over the rim of the mug they held clutched over my parched mouth.

Jett snorted with laughter.

"Oh for fucks sake," I rasped, grabbing the water glass out of their hands and chugging the water in four glorious swallows. At least half of it splashed onto my chin and neck, but that felt just as good as the stuff sliding down my throat. But it was only a drop compared to the raging thirst burning inside me. If anything, it had only gotten worse now that I'd had a few drops.

Owen jumped off the bed and slipped through the door without a word. My wolf whined with annoyance. But my human side was so parched I thought I'd shrivel up like a piece of Ariana jerky if I didn't get some water in the next ten seconds. As if hearing my thought, Owen appeared with another tall glass of water.

I wanted to thank him, but I didn't know if I had the energy to say two things, and my greedy side won. "I'm going to need more."

"Take it easy," Cash said, sinking onto the bed beside me. His black hair fell in tight curls around his handsome face. "You can have as much as you need, but drink it slowly. It won't help if you get sick and have to start all over."

Owen held the glass gently to my lips, and this time, I managed to swallow all the water instead of spilling half of it. My body yearned for more fluids, more coldness.

"It takes a lot out of you to breathe fire," Cash said. "You probably just overdid it your first time. If I'd known…"

Suddenly, a memory flashed in my mind. Falling. Shifting. Spewing flames.

Holy fucking shit. I was the blowtorch that had incinerated my throat.

"What?" I whispered, my throat feeling clearer despite my continued craving.

"If I'd known you could shift into a dragon, I would have trained you a little," Cash said. "I thought—we all thought—you were a wolf shifter."

I'd thought I was a wolf shifter. If I was more, shouldn't I have known all my life? I'd known I was a wolf for as long as I'd known I was human. Hell, I'd known I was a wolf during the years of fighting, when I'd almost forgotten I was human.

How was I just now finding out about this?

"Ari?" Owen prompted.

I realized they were all waiting for an answer, but I couldn't give them what they wanted. I didn't know how it had happened, either.

"I didn't know," I said at last. "It's never happened before."

"That'll do it, then," Cash said. "You need to know how to make fire so it won't burn you up and deplete you. Most of us start small and work our way up to bigger things."

"Like humans," I whispered, horrified at the memories swirling through me. People running across a rooftop, fleeing in terror. Holy shit, I'd eaten someone whole!

"Not humans," Max croaked beside me. "Vampires."

Right. I'd swallowed a vampire. There was literally a bloodsucker inside me. I held a hand to my stomach as it churned. Gross.

I turned to look at Max. He looked more tired than I felt. Then I remembered why I'd done it, why I'd shifted—why I'd killed those vamps. For him, my mate, who had been tortured and chained in silver. A rush of protective anger washed through me. Someone had fucked with the wrong girl's mate. He deserved to be swallowed whole like the worm he was.

"Are you okay?" I asked, stroking Max's chestnut hair away from his forehead.

"Fine," he growled, turning his face away. A muscle in his jaw jumped though, belying the pain he was really in.

"Why haven't you healed?" I asked.

"The silver slows it down," he said, still facing away from me.

Awww, he didn't want me to see him in a weakened state. It was kind of cute, especially since I was feeling better by the second. But I didn't want to embarrass him in front of the other guys, so I didn't push.

"How about that water now?" I asked, turning to Cash.

"I'll get a gallon," he said with a grin, sliding off the bed and loping out of the room.

"Maybe it's your Silver Shifter gift," Jett said from where he still leaned on the wall, seemingly unconcerned with my awakening. I knew he was my mate—my wolf didn't make mistakes—and I knew that Jett knew it, too. But he'd refused to be bonded to me through a blood exchange.

Owen, Max, and I turned to stare at him.

"What do you mean?" Owen asked.

Jett shrugged and started tapping on his phone screen again. "Maybe her Silver Shifter gift is to shift into something besides a wolf."

I fought my irritation that he was talking about me like I wasn't there. But that was the least of my concerns right now. "Wouldn't I have known about it before?" I asked. "Even if I didn't know it, haven't I always been the Silver Shifter?"

"Maybe it happened when you took them as mates," Jett said.

We remained silent as his words sank in. All I could think about was how he said I took them as mates. My wolf growled at being denied her fourth mate, but I couldn't imagine Jett ever letting me get close enough to kiss him, let alone doing a blood exchange. I couldn't pretend the rejection didn't sting, either. Not that I was any more anxious to get cuddly than he was. The others might challenge me at times, but Jett had been just plain dickish since the moment we met. My wolf, however, made no such distinctions. She found the sight of his hardened muscles, velvety brown skin, and sculpted jawline just as yummy as all the others'.

A minute later, Cash returned carrying a gallon jug of water as promised. "What did I miss?" he asked, his eyes moving from one of us to the next.

"Jett has an interesting theory," Owen said. "What if Ari gained powers from taking a mate?"

Jett snorted. "Try three. She took three mates."

"So maybe I have three powers," I said, ignoring Jett's pointed reminder that I'd gone against the rules of werewolf mating. I chose to believe that's what he was doing, not that he was rubbing it in that he was the lone hold-out.

"Can you shift into anything else?" Owen asked, his blue eyes hopeful. "Like a bear?"

"I could try," I said, though in truth, just talking was exhausting. "Let me have another drink first." I reached for the water in Cash's hand, my fingers trembling.

Owen supported the jug while I gulped down water until I could hear it sloshing in my stomach with every swallow. I was too tired to be embarrassed. God, I was tired.

I closed my eyes for a second and tried to feel another presence inside me. My wolf was strong—maybe stronger than my human side. She was happy to be surrounded by her mates, despite Cash's refusal to bond with me officially. My dragon, well, she was apparently happily sleeping. Ariana the human was supremely jealous of her.

No matter how I strained, I couldn't feel anything

else inside me. At last, I opened my eyes, my body just about melting with the effort I'd put in.

"There's nothing else," I said. "No other animals. Just my wolf, my dragon, and me."

"That must be a fun party," Jett said, smirking.

"No bear?" Owen asked, looking slightly wounded.

I shook my head, letting my eyes fall closed again.

"I thought that maybe, since you'd taken me as a mate, too…"

"I'm sorry," I whispered. Now that my thirst was sated for the moment at least, I wanted nothing more than to sleep for a week straight.

"That's enough excitement for the day," Max said. "You're going to wear her out if you keep pushing her."

"She took three mates," Jett said. "Shouldn't she expect to get worn out?"

"Get out," Max growled, pushing halfway up off the bed, his jaw clenched and his eyes flashing.

"I was already on my way," Jett said as he swaggered out of the room. I swear he had a little extra bounce in his step and a lot of laughter in his voice. The bastard.

"All of you," Max said, glaring at Cash and Owen. "We both need rest, and Ari doesn't need you hovering over her while she sleeps."

"You're right," Cash said. "I'll join the wolves in patrolling the pack's land. I can keep a lookout from the air."

"Feel better soon," Owen said, leaning over to kiss

my forehead. Our eyes met, and the warmth and concern in his gaze made my heart glow with warmth.

"I will," I whispered.

When the other two had left, Max rolled toward me and wrapped his arms around me. "Thank you," he whispered, nuzzling my ear.

"I should be thanking you," I said. "You got us some peace and quiet."

"You saved my life," Max said, his voice serious.

"You would have done the same for me."

"I would have," he said, inhaling my scent. "I would die for you, Ari."

I slid my arms around him, reveling in the strength of his embrace even when he was injured. I rested my head against his firm chest and closed my eyes. Despite his flaws, I knew in that moment that there was no one on earth who understood me better—who would protect me and anticipate my every need better than Maximus, my stubborn, prickly, beloved wolf mate.

Follow Ari and her mates in the next installment, coming April 9th.

# ABOUT KATHERINE BOGLE

Katherine Bogle is the bestselling author of the steampunk phenomenon, QUEEN OF THIEVES, as well as the international bestselling DOMINION RISING series.

She first found success with her debut novel, Haven, which came second in the World's Best Story contest 2015. Since then, she has gone on to release 11 books with one core theme: kick-butt heroines. Though her series may span genres—from fantasy, to steampunk to science fiction—she will always write about strong women overcoming the odds.

**Join her newsletter for info on upcoming releases, free stuff and more:**
https://www.subscribepage.com/p200e3

*Follow Katherine for all the latest updates:*
katherinebogle.com
AuthorKatherineBogle@outlook.com

## ABOUT ALEXA B. JAMES

Alexa B. James is the adult romance shared pen name for 2 USA Today Bestselling YA authors.

The Alexas love coffee and romance novels of every variety (why choose?). Their plans for world domination include writing more books that make your pulse pound and your heart sing.

**Join their newsletter for info on upcoming releases, free stuff and more:**
http://eepurl.com/dvkHYv

Made in the USA
San Bernardino, CA
26 July 2019